"For the first time I think I understand the arsonist..."

Sam's brow furrowed as she stared up at Braden. "How?"

"Sometimes you have a compulsion to do something and you just can't fight it..."

"You have a compulsion to set a fire?"

"I have a compulsion to do this..." He touched her—just his fingertips along her jaw. Her skin was so silky, just like her hair, which brushed across his hand. He tipped up her chin, and when he lowered his mouth to hers he felt a jolt.

Maybe she felt the jolt, too, because she gasped. And he deepened the kiss, dipping his tongue inside her mouth to taste her. She was sweet and sexy and hot as hell.

He felt the fire burning between them.

Then something flew through the open window, dropping onto the hardwood floor with a crash of breaking glass.

A Molotov cocktail.

Now there was a real fire burning in the house. And like his kissing Sam, it was quick to get out of control...

Dear Reader,

I hope you've been enjoying reading my Hotshot Heroes series for Harlequin Blaze as much as I've been enjoying writing the books. I've had so much fun with the Hotshots' camaraderie and with their resistance to falling in love. All of them have fallen but for one. Superintendent Braden Zimmer has the biggest reason for avoiding love. He's already been burned—badly—with a horrible marriage that ended in divorce. And now he's busy trying to track down the arsonist who's been terrorizing his hometown and home base of Northern Lakes, Michigan.

Sexy arson investigator Sam McRooney might solve one problem. If she's as good as her reputation, she'll catch the firebug who has now started sending Braden threatening notes. Or she might make herself the arsonist's next target... Braden wants to protect her. He also wants *her*—badly. But he has to resist, or risk being burned again. Please enjoy the exciting conclusion to this hot series!

Happy reading!

Lisa Childs

Lisa Childs

Hot Pursuit

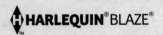

Recycling programs
for this product may
not exist in your area.

ISBN-13: 978-0-373-79951-0

Hot Pursuit

Copyright © 2016 by Lisa Childs

Printed in U.S.A.

Ever since **Lisa Childs** read her first romance novel (a Harlequin story, of course) at age eleven, all she wanted was to be a romance writer. With over forty novels published with Harlequin, Lisa is living her dream. She is an award-winning, bestselling romance author. Lisa loves to hear from readers, who can contact her on Facebook, through her website, lisachilds.com, or her snail-mail address, PO Box 139, Marne, MI 49435.

Books by Lisa Childs

Harlequin Blaze
Hotshot Heroes

Red Hot
Hot Attraction
Hot Seduction

Harlequin Romantic Suspense
Bachelor Bodyguards

His Christmas Assignment
Bodyguard Daddy
Bodyguard's Baby Surprise
Beauty and the Bodyguard

Harlequin Intrigue
Special Agents at the Altar

The Pregnant Witness
Agent Undercover
The Agent's Redemption

Shotgun Weddings

Groom Under Fire
Explosive Engagement
Bridegroom Bodyguard

To get the inside scoop on Harlequin Blaze and its talented writers, visit Facebook.com/BlazeAuthors.

All backlist available in ebook format.

Visit the Author Profile page at Harlequin.com for more titles.

With great appreciation for Laura Barth, my amazing editor, who helped me so much with writing this series! Thank you for your wonderful insight and support!

_1_

ANOTHER BIG FIRE was coming. Braden Zimmer didn't see or smell the smoke yet. He didn't hear the crackle and roar of the flames. But he _felt_ it—not the heat; he felt the certainty and the dread and the foreboding.

A fire was coming.

Unless he could stop it…

Unless he could stop the arsonist…

For months Braden, the superintendent of the Huron Hotshots, an elite team of US Forest Service firefighters, had been trying to find the person responsible for setting fires in his home base of Northern Lakes, Michigan. But he was no closer to nailing a suspect than he'd been when the first fire was set six months ago.

He wasn't giving up. He wouldn't stop looking until he found the person responsible for the fires. But he could no longer argue he didn't need help. Yet catching up an arson investigator from the US Forest Service who knew nothing about the case was going to take more time Braden didn't have.

Not when he was so certain another fire would be set soon. It wasn't just his instincts warning him about another blaze. It was the arsonist himself.

He glanced down at the note he'd found sitting on his desk in the Northern Lakes firehouse. There was no envelope. It hadn't been mailed; it had been placed on the scratched surface of his old metal desk. The son of a bitch had walked right into the firehouse—into Braden's office. Too bad they didn't have security cameras in the firehouse. But they had never needed them; until the fires, there had never been much crime in Northern Lakes. The arsonist had been getting bolder and bolder with each fire, but this was ridiculous.

The action taunted Braden as much as the note itself:

YOU MADE A TERRIBLE MISTAKE. AND IT'S GOING TO COST YOU AND YOUR TEAM GRAVELY...

Since the fires were only set when his team was in Northern Lakes, he'd already figured out it was personal. He just hadn't realized how personal—that he was the one the arsonist wanted to hurt the most.

Leaving the note where he'd found it, Braden pulled the office door shut behind him as he exited the room. This time he tested the knob, making sure it was locked. Few people locked their doors in Northern Lakes. Until the fires had started, it hadn't been necessary. Nothing bad had ever happened here, as far back as Braden could remember, and he'd been born and raised in the northeastern Michigan town. He'd only left for college.

He headed down the hall toward the workout room. Like his office, the hallway walls were concrete blocks—the floors bare concrete, too. But in the workout room there was a wall of mirrors behind the equipment. Ignoring his reflection, he settled onto the weight bench and began to lift. Despite not having to wield a chain saw or ax anymore like his team, he liked to make sure he still could. He wouldn't have their respect if he couldn't physically do the job he asked them to do. At thirty-three, he was one of the youngest Hotshot superintendents, so it was important that he maintained authority over his team.

That wasn't why he worked out now, though. He was trying to ease the frustration that had his stomach clenched into knots. Lifting the heavy bar up before lowering it nearly to his chest over and over again, he pushed himself—harder and harder. But instead of alleviating his tension, it elevated.

Some of his guys thought he just needed to get laid—that sex would ease his frustration. But Braden knew he needed to stop the arsonist. And he needed to do it soon.

Or that big fire would start…

Maybe it was already too late to stop it, since he could feel it coming. So far they'd been lucky. The Hotshots had been able to rescue everyone in harm's way; they'd been able to put out every blaze without any serious injuries.

But the arsonist had been getting more and more dangerous. Eventually someone was going to get hurt or killed. If he believed the warning in the note, that someone was going to be him—or worse, a member of his team.

They weren't just his workers or fellow firefighting Hotshots. They were his family. He couldn't lose any of them.

SAM MCROONEY WALKED through the open garage door of the Northern Lakes firehouse. In the three-story cement-block building with its bright red metal roof, she could almost smell the testosterone. She'd grown up in a houseful of males, so she was accustomed to it. As an arson investigator for the US Forest Service, she was used to dealing with macho men. But Hotshots were another breed entirely—the macho-est of the macho. They were the firefighters who risked life and limb, battling the blaze on the front line.

"Hello?" she called out. Her voice echoed hollowly off the concrete floors and walls. She knew they weren't out west fighting wildfires right now—not without their superintendent. And Zimmer was here; he'd called in the arsonist's threat just over an hour ago. He knew she was coming. Was he avoiding her?

The firefighters weren't out on a local call, either. The garage was full, an engine—the same bright yellow as the Hotshots uniforms—in every bay. And in the lot next to the firehouse, she'd parked beside a black US Forest Service pickup truck. Somebody had to be here. Or else why had the door been left open?

If they were that careless, they were lucky the arsonist had just left a note. He could have burned down the firehouse.

"Hello?" she called out again as she stepped farther inside the garage.

Instead of her voice, she heard the echo of a door slamming from somewhere above her. She quickly climbed the steps. At the top of the landing, she started down the wide hallway. The sound had come from up here; someone was in the building. Someone besides her.

Maybe the arsonist had returned to burn down the firehouse, after all. She reached for the weapon she was carrying in her purse since her gun belt was in her duffel bag along with her uniform. She usually wore the tan-and-green US Forest Service uniform, but as an arson investigator, she could dress in plainclothes, too. She withdrew the Glock and moved slowly down the hallway. Maybe she was overreacting, but she would rather be cautious than careless.

"Anyone here?" she called out.

Hinges creaked as a door opened; steam billowed into the hall. Then a man stepped out. Water dripped from his short dark hair and glistened on his broad shoulders and naked chest. He wore only a towel, cinched low on his lean hips. He lifted his hands, and the towel slipped a little lower.

"Are you holding me up?" he asked, and a slight grin curved his mouth.

She shook her head. "I'm with the US Forest Service."

"Me, too," he said. "You don't need the gun."

He obviously wasn't armed. But she wasn't convinced he wasn't dangerous. He was making her heart race, her palms sweat. She tightened her grip on her weapon, but then slid it back into her purse.

He lowered his hands, and just as it had begun to slip free from his hips, he caught the towel and secured it.

Ignoring the flash of disappointment she felt, she explained her reason for pulling her gun, the strange feeling she'd had as she'd walked into the firehouse. "The big door was open, but nobody was around."

"Nobody?" he asked.

"I didn't know you were up here…" In the shower. Naked. But now that she knew, she could imagine it, could imagine him standing under the water, his impressive muscles rippling beneath the pulsating spray. "…until I heard the door."

"That damn kid," he muttered. "He should have been down there washing trucks."

"I'm not here to meet with some kid," she said. At least no Hotshot superintendent she'd ever met had been a kid. "I'm here to meet with Superintendent Zimmer."

"I'm sorry," he said. "I'm Braden Zimmer. I would

have been downstairs, but I thought it was going to take longer for someone to get here from the chief's office."

It would have taken longer—had she not already been on her way north to investigate. "I was in the area," she said. "You're Zimmer?" He wasn't a kid, but he was younger than most superintendents she'd met.

He nodded, and water droplets sprayed from his hair onto her face. "Yeah." He reached out and, with the pad of his thumb, wiped the droplets from her cheek. "Sorry. I didn't mean to get you wet."

She narrowed her eyes and studied his handsome face. As a female working in a still male-dominated field, she endured more than her share of sexual innuendo. But there was no flirtatious smile or teasing glint in his dark eyes. He had no idea there could have been a double entendre in his words. It was good he wasn't a flirt. And that he had no idea how he—and his near nakedness—had affected her.

She fought to steady her pulse and cool her skin, which had heated even more from the touch of his hand. She'd also felt an unexpected tingling sensation. But that was silly.

She was around guys who looked like him all the time. Hell, she was around even younger, hotter guys. And while she appreciated their masculine beauty, she never reacted to it. And she sure as hell never let them get to her.

"I'm Sam McRooney," she said as she extended her hand to him.

"McRooney?" he repeated as he closed his hand around hers.

The sensation jolted her again; it reminded her of when her brothers had tricked her into reaching for a piece of shock gum. As her fingers had closed around the foil-covered stick, an electrical charge would travel from the tips up her arm. Braden Zimmer was exactly like shock gum.

"Are you related to Mack McRooney?" he asked the inevitable question everyone asked when they heard her last name. Her father was a legend for all the years he'd been a smoke jumper and for all the smoke jumpers he'd trained and led.

She nodded. "He's my dad."

Braden cocked his head. "I thought he had all boys."

"I have four brothers." She wished she hadn't been the only female. She'd spent her entire life having to prove she was as strong and capable as the boys.

"Maybe it's because of your name," Zimmer explained.

No. It was probably because her father never talked about her like he did her brothers. Like all of them, she'd started out as a firefighter. But she hadn't been tall enough or strong enough to become a smoke jumper or a Hotshot. So she'd focused on fighting fires another way— at the source. She'd wanted to stop them from starting at all—by stopping arsonists. She'd worked hard, taking college courses in criminal investigations and psychology along with specialized arson programs. And it had paid off. At twenty-seven she was one of the top investigators with the US Forest Service.

Why didn't her father brag about that?

"Is Sam short for Samantha?" Zimmer added.

She shook her head. "No." She wished. But her father had named each of his kids for one of the men he'd trained and lost to a fire. Eventually some women had become smoke jumpers, too, stronger, taller women than her—but not until after Sam's birth.

"You're a long way from Washington," Braden said.

He was probably referring to the state—where her father lived. But she wasn't there anymore.

"Michigan's not far from DC," she said, which was where she lived now. But she felt like it was far away—like she was going someplace she'd never gone before. She tugged on her hand, which he still held, yet in a loose grasp, as if he'd forgotten he was holding it.

"Sorry," he murmured. Then he glanced down at his bare chest. "I—I really should get dressed."

She nodded. But she wasn't certain she agreed. While a dressed Braden Zimmer would be less distracting, she enjoyed looking at him—looking at all those sculpted muscles.

"Yes," she agreed. "You get dressed. I can look over the letter from the arsonist while you do."

"It's locked in my office. I'll get it for you after I…" He pushed open the door to the locker room.

"Get dressed," she finished for him and nodded again. But it would be a shame to cover up all that masculine perfection.

"Are you just picking it up for the arson investigator?" he asked.

She tensed, but not with attraction now. Chauvinists were never particularly appealing to her. Maybe that was why she hadn't previously been attracted to any of the good-looking macho types she'd met, though they were often attracted to her. She always adopted a certain tone and attitude in order to fend them off. She didn't need to fend off Braden Zimmer. But she needed to let him know she wouldn't tolerate his chauvinism.

So she used that tone now, her voice going all icy, as she informed him, "I *am* the arson investigator."

2

As HE STEPPED out of the locker room, Braden fumbled with the buttons on his shirt. He had dressed in a hurry. But it was already too late. He hadn't just gotten caught with his pants down; he'd gotten caught with them off.

Not that he'd been doing anything wrong. He hadn't been expecting anyone from the US Fire Service to show up so quickly. And he certainly hadn't been expecting Sam McRooney.

Mack's daughter. And she didn't just work for the US Fire Service like her Hotshot, smoke jumper and ranger brothers, she was the arson investigator.

And he was a fool for not realizing it sooner.

Clearly, he wasn't the only one who thought him foolish, either. The way she'd looked at him when she'd informed him who she was...

He shivered, and it wasn't because his skin was still damp from the shower. She'd frozen him out.

He found her at the bottom of the stairs. She wasn't alone. Stanley had returned from wherever he'd gone, and he'd brought that damn dog with him. Someone had dropped off the puppy at the firehouse a few months ago. Orphan Annie, as they'd named her, was probably part

sheepdog and part mastiff; she was huge and hairy and—
if Braden believed one of his Hotshots—heroic. She was
also standing with her paws on the arson investigator's
slender shoulders. And the dog probably weighed more
than the petite blonde.

"Stanley," he admonished the kid. "Get Annie off Ms.
McRooney."

The curly-haired teenager tucked his fingers beneath
the dog's collar and pulled her down.

"Where were you earlier?" Braden asked the kid. "I
asked you to watch the firehouse while I took a shower.
But you took off and left it wide open." Which probably
also explained how the arsonist had waltzed right in earlier and left that note on his desk.

Stanley's face flushed a bright red. "I'm sorry, Superintendent Zimmer. Annie ran off after a cat, and I had to
catch her before she got hurt."

"What about the cat?" the woman asked.

"Annie wouldn't hurt anything or anyone," Stanley
defended the dog. "But she could've been hit by a car."

Braden nodded. "Okay, I understand." Occasionally
he had to reprimand the kid—like when Stanley talked
to reporters or ignored orders to drop a puppy at the hu-
mane society. But Braden usually wound up feeling worse
than he made Stanley feel. "If you have to leave again,
please close down the door, though. I will be in my office with Ms. McRooney—"

"Ms. McRooney?" Stanley interrupted. He probably
recognized the last name. Her father had nearly gotten
the boy's foster brother to leave Northern Lakes.

"Sam," she said.

Wanting to get the meeting back on track, Braden told
the kid, "Sam and I will be in my office."

She glanced at him, and those blue eyes were still cool.

She must have only been giving Stanley permission to use her first name—not him.

Braden led the way—through the garage and down the hall, past the workout room to his office. He fumbled with the ring of keys clipped to his hip until he found the right one.

"Don't often lock it?" she asked.

He shook his head.

"I can see how the arsonist got in—"

He flinched.

And she added "—easily."

He pushed open the door, but when she moved to pass through ahead of him, he caught her arm and stopped her. She glanced down at his hand on her arm, then looked up at his face. He shivered again at the coldness of her gaze.

"I am not a chauvinist," he told her, his pride prickling that she obviously thought he was. "When I called the chief's office, they told me it could take a while for an arson investigator to get here. That's why I didn't think you were the investigator."

"When they called, I was closer to Northern Lakes than they thought I would be."

He wanted to ask where she'd been. But he wanted to resolve their misunderstanding first. "And I know your dad," he continued. "He always brags about his boys being Hotshots and smoke jumpers and rangers. So I thought you were a ranger."

She flinched now. "I'm not a boy."

There was no mistaking Sam McRooney for a man—not with her petite but curvy body. Her waist was tiny but her hips swelled into a tightly rounded derriere cradled in tight-fitting jeans. He'd never realized he was an ass man until now. Her silky blond hair was short, barely falling to the shoulders of her pale blue sweater, but the yellow locks framed a delicately featured face. She was quite beautiful.

"I know," he assured her.

"Sometimes my dad forgets."

Braden bet her father was the only man who made that mistake. But then he wondered if she meant her dad forgets she's female or forgets about her entirely.

"I wish other people would forget I was female," she admitted. "Too many question my ability to do my job merely because of my sex."

Braden shook his head. "Sex has nothing to do with it."

She arched a blond brow. "Really?"

"I can't speak for anyone else," he said. "But for me, sex doesn't matter."

Her lips curved into a wider smile, and a twinkle brightened her blue eyes. Then he realized what he'd said. And he hoped like hell none of his men had overheard it. They would all mercilessly tease him, especially Cody Mallehan and Wyatt Andrews. Those two Hotshots were always giving each other a hard time, and since his divorce, they'd been on a mission to lighten him up and get him laid.

"That's not what I meant," he said.

"I know," she said. "You're trying to assure me you're not a chauvinist."

"I'm not," he said. "I have two female crew members who work every bit as hard as the guys. They've earned my respect."

"Why did they have to earn it?"

"Everyone does," he said with a shrug. It had always been that way; he'd had to prove himself, too, or he wouldn't have had the job he did. "You have to prove yourself, too."

"Oh, I've done that," she said. "The Brynn County wildfire… I caught the arsonist."

He expelled a breath. "That was you?"

She nodded.

Maybe the chief had sent the right investigator. "That fire was a few years ago," he said. "You look so young I didn't realize you've been on the job that long."

She emitted a shaky sigh, and he felt the sweet caress of it against his throat. They were still standing in the doorway—too close. "I thought you were too young, too," she admitted with a sheepish smile.

"Too young?" Already married and divorced, he felt old—older than his thirty-three years. And after dealing with the threat of the arsonist, he felt even older.

"Too young to be a Hotshot superintendent," she said. "I didn't think you were Braden Zimmer when we met in the hallway."

"Maybe I look younger in just a towel," he said.

Her lips parted on a soft gasp, and her eyes darkened as her pupils dilated. Her skin flushed. Then she *finally* stepped away from him and settled into one of the chairs in front of his desk.

Was she embarrassed? He was the one who should have been embarrassed.

"Sorry about that," he said as he dropped into the chair behind his desk.

"I know," she said. "You didn't expect me to show up as quickly as I had."

"Where were you?" he asked.

"Already on my way here," she said.

He cocked his head. Did she have a sixth sense, too? How had she known he was going to call? So far the US Forest Service had been letting him and the state police handle the arson investigation. "Why?"

"My dad is Mack McRooney," she reminded him. "He respects you and also thinks highly of a Hotshot named Cody Mallehan. Mack's concerned about all of you and asked me to look into the fires."

"Mack tried to poach Cody from me," Braden said with mock resentment. "Recruit him as a smoke jumper."

She smiled. "The way he tells the story, he only lent you Cody, and you won't give him back."

Braden chuckled. "I could see how he might see it that way." Since that was the way it had actually been.

"Lucky for you Mack doesn't hold a grudge."

"You call him Mack?" he asked. "To his face?" If he called either of his parents by their first names, Ben and Ramona would kick his butt even now.

She nodded. "He prefers it. My brothers and I have always called him Mack."

He suspected she'd had an interesting upbringing. "And your mom allowed that?"

She shrugged. "She didn't stick around to protest."

And now he remembered hearing that Mack had raised his kids alone. But nobody had ever said if his wife had died. Apparently she'd just left, deserting her husband and her kids.

Sam had had a very interesting upbringing then. He wanted to ask her more. But she was pointing toward the note on his desk. "Is that it?"

Braden suppressed a groan. He'd rather talk about her than the arsonist. He already talked about the fire-starter entirely too much with his team. But he never got any closer to discovering who he was. Maybe Sam could actually help. She had caught the Brynn County arsonist, after all.

He touched the edge of the paper, but she reached across the desk and caught his wrist. "Don't…"

He didn't mind her touching him. In fact he kind of enjoyed it—enjoyed the sensation of her fingertips sliding over his skin. But it wasn't necessary for her to stop him. She moved her hand from his. Then she stood up and moved around the desk until she stood behind him.

"You won't find any fingerprints on it," he said. "The state police didn't find any on the notes he left for Avery Kincaid."

"She's the reporter," Sam said. "The one who did the special feature on your assistant superintendent Dawson Hess."

He nodded, and his head nearly bumped hers as she leaned over his shoulder. Her breath whispered across his cheek as she read, "'You made a terrible mistake…'"

He felt her gaze on his face, as if she was speculating what that mistake might have been. He waited for her to ask. But instead she continued to read, "'And it's going to cost you—'"

The mistakes he'd made had already cost him.

"'—and your team gravely…'"

He flinched. He didn't care about himself as much as his team. It was his responsibility to make sure they were safe. Working fires like they did, they were in enough danger without a psychopath targeting them.

Her breath whistled between her teeth and brushed warmly across his ear. He nearly shivered at the sensation. He hadn't been this close to a woman in quite a while—not since the drunk women who'd tried to tear off his clothes some months ago. That would teach him for letting Wyatt Andrews talk him into checking out some new club—one that had featured male exotic dancers on the night they'd gone. Braden had fended the women off then, but he suspected he wouldn't fight Sam McRooney too hard if she had the inclination to undress him.

"Mack was right to be concerned," she remarked.

Braden uttered a ragged sigh of resignation. She was Mack's daughter. And Mack was a friend. Braden wouldn't cross that line with her even if she wasn't the US Forest Service arson investigator.

"You're in danger," she said.

"We already knew the arsonist was fixated on us," Braden said. "The fires only happen when we're in Northern Lakes. He's gone after a couple of my men directly."

"Cody Mallehan," she said. "The arsonist cut his brake line and sabotaged a shower, making him slip. He got a concussion out of that."

Braden added, "He went after Cody's girlfriend, Serena Beaumont, too."

"Her boardinghouse was burned down."

Maybe he shouldn't have worried about wasting time bringing Sam McRooney up to speed. She obviously knew quite a bit about the fires.

"Just like he burned down Avery Kincaid's cottage," she continued. "He's targeting your superintendents and the women they're seeing."

Braden's stomach clenched with dread. If Dawson had lost Avery or Cody had lost Serena…

He would have lost his men as well. They would have gone out of their minds if such amazing women had been taken from their lives.

"Are you seeing anyone?" she asked.

Braden turned his head, and his mouth nearly brushed across her cheek. Her eyes dilated, the pupils swallowing up the blue until it just rimmed the black. She jerked back.

"Why would you ask that?" He doubted she was interested in him. As beautiful as she was, she was probably already seeing someone.

"Because the arsonist appears to be targeting you now," she pointed out.

He glanced down at the note. And he couldn't argue with her.

"If you're seeing anyone, she would be in danger, too."

Because of the arsonist, Braden hadn't had the time or the inclination to date anyone—despite how some members of his team had pushed him into socializing after his divorce. But apparently that was a good thing, because if he had gotten involved with anyone, he'd have only put the woman in danger.

"I just got divorced…" A year ago. It had been a year. The revelation stunned him. No wonder his men were pressuring him to get back out there. It had been a while. "So no, I'm not seeing anyone."

"That's good," Sam said, and she looked away from him, as if unwilling to meet his gaze.

His heart rate accelerated. Was she interested? Not that anything could come of it…

But it was nice to know that women didn't have to be drunk in order to find him attractive.

"Now we only have to worry about protecting you," she continued.

"Protecting me?"

"Yes, you're obviously the arsonist's next target," she said. Her brow furrowed slightly. "Or maybe you've been his ultimate target all along. So we need to make sure you have protection—around the clock."

"Who?" Braden asked. "You? Are you going to protect me, Sam?"

He was just teasing. Even though she carried a gun,

she was an arson investigator—not a bodyguard. He expected her to use that icy tone and remind him as much.

Instead she replied, simply and succinctly, "Yes."

Maybe she meant well or she was only trying to please her father, but Braden couldn't allow her to get that close to him. As she had just pointed out, any woman who got close to him would be risking her life.

3

SAM INTENDED TO protect Braden Zimmer—by stopping the Northern Lakes arsonist. It wasn't going to be easy, though. In fact it felt a lot like when her brothers had gotten a head start on her in a game of tag. It hadn't mattered that they were older and stronger. Eventually she'd caught them, though—just like she'd catch the arsonist. And maybe it would be the same way. Her brothers had let her catch them. The arsonist wanted to be caught. She could see that in his notes. He wanted the notoriety, but he also wanted to be stopped—at least subconsciously. He probably wasn't aware that his letters were a cry for help.

"I wish you would've called for help sooner," she remarked as she walked across the charred ground in the Huron National Forest. On the other side of the dirt road on which Braden had parked the US Forest Service black pickup, the trees were vibrant with yellow, orange and red leaves. Where they stood, the sparse trees that remained were bare of leaves, their trunks as black as the ground beneath them.

Braden sighed. "I was working it alongside the state police. I thought we'd have caught him by now."

"You were busy working other fires," she reminded

him. "This is all I do." But she'd started out fighting fires, too, before she'd taken the special training to become an arson investigator.

He ran his hand through his thick brown hair. It had dried now and looked so soft Sam was tempted to touch it. But she curled her fingers into her palm.

"We still should have caught him by now," Braden remarked.

"We'll catch him soon," she promised. She flipped through the photos on her tablet. She had pictures of every crime scene. "This is the place where it started."

"Yes," Braden replied, though she hadn't asked a question. "The first fire was traced back to this spot."

She glanced around, studying the blackened area. "He restarted it a few times since…"

Braden slid his hand around the nape of his neck and squeezed as if trying to relieve some tension. "More than a few—it's like he's determined for the forest to stay dead."

"This area was already slated for a prescribed burn," she deduced.

Braden's dark eyes widened in surprise. Then he glanced at her tablet. "Were you told that? Is that in the records you have?"

She shook her head. Nobody had bothered writing it into the report. "I grew up in the middle of a national forest," she said.

Her father had raised her and brothers in a US Forest Service cabin. The structure had been small—one bedroom for her dad and a loft in which she and her brothers had all slept on mattresses on the floor. But they had never spent much time inside; their home had been the forest itself. "Mack taught me about burns and breaks before I learned my ABCs."

Braden's mouth curved into a slight grin, drawing her attention and making her wonder what it might be like to kiss his lips. "Mack knows his stuff..."

And he'd taught his children well—all about the ways of getting burned. Professionally and personally.

She turned her attention back to the crime scene. Her only interest in Braden Zimmer was getting whatever information he had about the arsonist. Not how he looked in a towel, or how his hair might feel, how his mouth might taste...

She shook off the fanciful thoughts. Maybe she'd been working too much—trying too hard to prove herself. And for what? Even catching the Brynn County arsonist hadn't been impressive enough for Mack to mention to his friends. And she doubted her brothers talked about her at all...

Once she found this arsonist she would reward herself with a mini-vacation. But for now she had a job to do—and a criminal to catch.

"The arsonist seems to know his stuff, too," she said. "I don't think he intended to do the damage he did with the first fire." That was why he'd started it where one was already intended to happen. But how had he known that?

Braden snorted. "He nearly killed a bunch of Boy Scouts." Then he shuddered. "And a few of my guys..."

"That was just because it was unseasonably dry and the fire took off," she said. "I don't think that had been his intention with the first one."

"Do you have photos of the others?" he asked as he stepped closer behind her. Since he was so much taller than her, it was easy for him to look over her shoulder.

She could feel the heat of his body against her back and her butt. She forgot what he'd asked her.

He didn't wait for her to remember. He reached over

her shoulder and touched the screen of her tablet. His arm brushed against hers, then fleetingly grazed her breast as he scrolled through the photos.

She held her breath but studied the photos. A cottage, its once-light-teal vertical siding blackened. A couple of photos later, the cottage was nearly gone.

"The fire wasn't bad the first time," Braden said. "So he came back. He nearly killed Avery Kincaid."

"He left threatening notes on her doorstep," Sam said, moving her finger across the screen until a photo of the notes was displayed. Her finger brushed against Braden's, and she felt that disturbing jolt again.

He slid his finger across the screen, flipping through more photos. "He's inconsistent, though. He didn't leave any notes for Serena," he said, anger rumbling in his deep voice. "He just torched the house, nearly killing her and her boarders."

She glanced up at his face, which was so close to hers. A muscle twitched along Braden's tightly clenched jaw.

"Maybe with this first fire he didn't mean to hurt anyone," Braden said. "But that quickly changed."

Sam couldn't argue that—not when she saw the photos of the houses. There had been even less left of the boardinghouse than the cottage. And Sam had seen photos of Serena Beaumont's historic home before the fire. It had been a huge, plantation-style estate that had served as a former stagecoach stop.

"He has done a lot of damage," Sam agreed.

"He is targeting people," Braden said, his voice rough with emotion. "My guys, their girlfriends…" He'd obviously taken it personally even before the arsonist left the threatening note.

Sam was beginning to wonder just how personal it was. Did the arsonist have a grudge against Braden Zimmer? Was it someone close to him? Someone maybe he trusted too much to suspect?

"Now he's targeting you," she reminded him.

"Good," Braden said. "Better me than anyone else."

She peered up at his handsome face. His square jaw, already dark with stubble, was rigid with determination. She wondered if he was just displaying macho bravado like her brothers always did. She was just looking at photos; Braden had seen the arsonist's destruction first-hand. He'd helped fight those fires. How could he not be afraid?

Sam was afraid for him. She had to catch the arsonist before he struck again.

"WHAT'S HE DOING HERE?" Braden asked as he noted the state police car parked outside as he drove up to the fire-house. For once Stanley had listened. The overhead doors were down, and since Trooper Gingrich sat in his vehicle instead of Braden's office, the other doors must have been locked as well.

"I called him," Sam said from the passenger seat.

"You already know more than he does about the investigation," Braden said.

Trooper Gingrich had been assigned to investigate the fires, but he hadn't gotten any closer to discovering who was responsible than Braden had. Just how hard had he actually tried, though? They'd argued with each other more than they'd collaborated.

Braden should have asked the US Forest Service to take over the investigation months ago. Sam was certainly a lot better-looking than the bald-headed trooper who stepped out of his vehicle.

"I called him to protect you," she said.

"I don't need a bodyguard," he said, though when he'd

thought she was volunteering for the position, he had momentarily been tempted to accept. But risking her life for his was out of the question. If anything happened to her, he was sure Mack would kill him. And even though he'd just met her, Braden would be beside himself with guilt and regret.

"The arsonist proved he doesn't make idle threats," Sam said.

Braden was well aware of that. He'd almost lost Dawson Hess and Cody Mallehan when they'd gone into burning houses without wearing protective gear, to rescue the women they loved. Fortunately both Avery and Serena had survived. If anything had happened to them, it would have destroyed two of Braden's best Hotshots. They loved those women so much. Braden thought he'd loved his ex-wife like that, but now he knew better—after witnessing real love. Ami had hurt his pride more than his heart when she'd left him for another man.

"You need to take his threat seriously," Sam persisted.

"It's not him I'm having trouble taking seriously," he murmured as the trooper approached Braden's pickup truck.

A breath hissed through Sam's teeth.

He cursed. Now she'd be thinking again that he was a chauvinist. "I'm not talking about you," he assured her as he pushed open the driver's door and stepped out.

"Zimmer," Trooper Gingrich greeted him coolly. Then he turned his attention to where Sam alighted from the passenger side. He stretched his hand out to her. "Ms. McRooney?"

She nodded and took his hand.

The trooper introduced himself as he held on to her. "I'm glad you gave me a call," he said. "I would really like to discuss the investigation with you."

She pulled her hand free of his grasp. "Of course. But first we need to get some more troopers patrolling Northern Lakes."

Braden couldn't argue against more patrols—not after receiving that threat. The arsonist was bound to set another fire. And Braden's instincts—which had never failed him professionally—were warning it would be soon.

"Have you already pinpointed a suspect?" the trooper asked with a glance at Braden, who kept his attention on Sam.

The last rays of the setting sun played across her face, making her skin look even more golden and her blue eyes brighter. She was beautiful—with delicate features. She must have resembled her mother because she looked nothing like her father. No wonder Mack hadn't mentioned having a daughter; he'd probably been trying to protect her from all the rabble-rousing firefighters he knew.

She shook her head, and that silky blond hair skimmed her jaw. "Not yet," she conceded. "But earlier he dropped off a threat to the firehouse. And if he's following the same MO that he did with Avery Kincaid, then he's going to act again—soon."

She was right. If the arsonist followed the same pattern he had with Avery, then he wouldn't wait for Braden to heed his warning. He was going to strike at any moment.

Braden wasn't afraid, though. He was anxious. He wanted the arsonist to make a move so they'd have an opportunity to catch him in the act.

"Of course he's going to start another fire," the trooper agreed. "Zimmer's team is back in town. There's a fire every time they're here."

Braden flinched. "Not every time," he called Gingrich out on his exaggeration.

"Maybe I should have said the fires only happen when his team is in town then," the trooper amended.

Braden heard the insinuation.

Sam must have heard it, too, because her heavily lashed eyes narrowed. "That's why you need extra troopers in the area," she said. "Superintendent Zimmer and his team are in danger."

The trooper shot Braden a resentful glare. He probably hated that Braden had called in the threat to the US Forest Service rather than the state police this time. "Are they in danger?" the trooper asked. "Or are they the danger?"

"What the hell are you implying?" Braden asked. He closed the distance between him and the trooper and stared down into the shorter man's flushed face.

"I'm not implying anything," the trooper said. "I'm only saying what everyone else in town has been saying…"

Dread tightened his stomach into knots. "And what's that?" Braden demanded to know.

"That this town is a hell of a lot safer when you and your team are gone," Gingrich said.

Since the fires had only happened when the Hotshots were in Northern Lakes, Braden found it hard to argue that point. But he didn't think that was all Gingrich was saying.

"You called us the danger," he pointed out. "We're not the ones setting fires."

The trooper raised his brow so high it disappeared beneath the brim of his hat, which he wore low, probably so Sam wouldn't see he'd already lost his hair. And he was only Braden's age.

In fact, they'd gone to school together. But they'd always been more rivals than friends—competing for the captain position for every team they'd played on together. Marty hadn't taken it well when he'd lost to Braden— which had happened a lot.

Braden had foolishly thought since they were adults now, they would be able to work together to find the arsonist. He should have known better, known Marty would argue everything.

"Are you accusing me of something?" he asked.

"No accusation," Marty said. "Just a logical conclusion. If the fires are only set when you and your team are in town, it stands to reason someone on your team is setting the fires."

It had been a long day—so long Braden's usually tight control slipped. Anger heated his blood and had it pumping fast and hard in his veins; he could hear the rush inside his head.

"Don't you dare," he warned the trooper. "Don't you damn well dare accuse one of my team members of setting fires—not after all the times they've risked their lives putting them out!"

"They're just like you," Gingrich said with a derisive snort. "Always playing the hero. Maybe one of them—" he stared hard up at Braden, making it clear which one he thought "—is making sure he has the opportunity to act like a hero."

A curse slipped through Braden's lips as his temper snapped entirely. And he reached for the trooper with one hand while he pulled his other one back and fisted it. Before he could take a swing at the guy's smug face, his elbow struck something else—someone who'd come up behind him.

And he cursed again. Sam pushed herself between

him and Gingrich, shoving Braden back. "Calm down,"
she yelled. And he noticed the red mark on her cheek.

He'd been worried about the wrong person hurting her.
He'd thought the arsonist would, but Braden was the one
who'd actually injured her. He reached for her face, but
she flinched and stepped back.

What the hell had he done?

4

"YOU NEED TO press charges," the trooper told Sam.

She hated being told what to do, which was another reason she never got involved with any of the alpha males she encountered in her profession. They were all too damn bossy. And hot-tempered—like Braden Zimmer.

Sure, Gingrich had been goading him. But the trooper wasn't wrong to question the involvement of one of the Hotshots. She'd noticed, too, that the fires occurred only when they were in Northern Lakes. When they were gone, nothing happened. She doubted that was just a coincidence—but was it because they were behind it? Or because they were being targeted?

"Press charges? For an accident?" she scoffed, shaking her head. Her cheek throbbed.

But she could tell she didn't feel as bad as Braden did. He stared at her solemnly from across the tavern. The Filling Station was just around the corner from the firehouse. It was a blue-collar bar with peanuts strewn across the floor. Braden had already apologized—profusely— and had offered to go into the firehouse to get an ice pack for her.

Trooper Gingrich had wanted to take her to the state

police post so she could press charges. She'd assured them both that she was fine. Then Braden had suggested coming here—for that ice pack.

Gingrich had insisted on coming along, and he'd been so obnoxious Sam had worried he'd provoke Braden into taking another swing. So she'd told Braden to let her talk to the trooper alone. He'd reluctantly left her—to join a few guys in a back booth near the pool tables. But just moments later, a confused waitress had brought her an ice pack.

She knew who had ordered it for her. Gingrich hadn't even offered to buy her a drink. But that was good. She didn't want a blowhard like him interested in her.

"I'm not the one Braden wanted to hit," she said.

"He's a hothead."

She would have agreed after how she'd seen him act just moments ago. But his anger had quickly evaporated. So she suspected he wasn't really as quick-tempered as he'd briefly appeared. He was just a man who had been under a lot of pressure for a long time, and Trooper Gingrich had purposely added to Braden's stress until it was too much for anyone to endure.

"I've never heard that about him," she said. Her father had told her quite a bit about Braden Zimmer when he'd asked if she was investigating the Northern Lakes fires. Of course Mack had no problem singing the praises of the men he'd worked with; it was her praises he never sang.

"I've known him a long time," Gingrich said, his puffy face flushing with anger. "We went to school together."

She narrowed her eyes to study the trooper's face, but the skin pulled on her swollen cheek and she flinched.

It was her fault she'd gotten hit. She knew better than to get between two angry alpha males. And if she was ever tempted to forget, she could just look at some of the scars she'd gotten for her efforts to stop her brothers from fighting. Though, like Braden, her brothers had always felt bad when she'd gotten hurt.

Gingrich didn't feel bad—despite his goading—that she'd gotten hurt. In fact he'd been smirking right afterward, and now that smirk curled his thin lips again. "I know more about Braden Zimmer than he knows himself…"

"Really?" she prompted him. "What do you know?"

His face flushed a deeper red, and he shook his head. "Nothing to do with the fires…"

"You pretty much accused him of setting them," she said. As a former firefighter herself, she knew how angry that would make her. Maybe she shouldn't have tried to stop that fight. But if Braden had struck Gingrich, she had no doubt the trooper would have immediately arrested him for assaulting an officer.

Gingrich snorted. "He's the most obvious suspect."

She tilted her head and considered it. She had already begun to suspect that a Huron Hotshot could be the arsonist. But the superintendent? Risking the lives of the team he'd seemed so passionate about protecting?

Not that she hadn't been lied to and misled before…

"Come on, you see it, too," Gingrich said patronizingly, as if she would be an idiot if she didn't.

"But what evidence do you have?" she asked, because she had seen nothing in the state police file. There had been photos of the crime scenes but no evidence that pointed to a suspect—any suspect.

"Do you have eyewitnesses who saw him in the area right before any of the fires?" she asked. She knew he'd been in the vicinity afterward because he and his team had put them out. "Do you have copies of any receipts you can trace back to him for the purchase of gasoline or hay bales?"

The trooper's face reddened an even darker shade. "If I had anything like that, I would have arrested him by now," he said, his voice still condescending.

"So you have no evidence," she concluded. "What exactly do you have against Braden Zimmer?"

"I—I don't— It's not like that," the guy stammered. "He's just…"

Better than him. Taller. More handsome. Smarter. Stronger. She knew guys like Gingrich—guys who'd hated her brothers just because of who they were. Of how effortlessly they'd been good at everything.

While she'd never hated her brothers, she had resented them from time to time. She'd definitely resented not being as strong as they were. Because of her small size, she had barely made the requirements to be a US Forest Service firefighter. She hadn't been big enough to make a Hotshot team or to become a smoke jumper. She wasn't physically capable of packing one hundred and ten pounds for ninety minutes—that would have been like carrying her own body weight. But her small stature wasn't her brothers' fault; she couldn't blame them.

Just how much did the trooper resent Braden? Enough to try to get back at him by starting those fires? She leaned a little closer and studied Martin Gingrich's flushed face. In addition to the arson-investigation courses, she had a degree in criminal psychology. She'd also attended seminars on FBI profiling at Quantico.

"Go on," she prodded. "Braden Zimmer is what?"

Gingrich leaned back and forced a nervous-sounding chuckle. "A psychic—if you believe him. He claims he's got some sixth sense about when a fire's coming." He snorted again, derisively.

Sam couldn't be so dismissive. Her father had that sixth sense—about people. He could read them so well. He'd once told her she'd inherited that ability from him— when she'd caught the Brynn County arsonist—but she wasn't as good as he was. She had made her share of mistakes over the years.

Like Chad. And Blake…

She flinched again, but not because of the pain in her cheek. Chad had reinforced her determination to stay away from alpha males. And Blake had proven beta males could be jerks, too. She wouldn't make those mistakes again. It was smarter to focus on her job—and at the moment that job was catching the Northern Lakes arsonist.

"I take it you're a nonbeliever?" she remarked.

"I don't believe in that psychic hocus-pocus stuff," he said. "I've been to the freak show at the carnival and wasted five bucks on some chain-smoking fortune-teller predicting my future. It never happened. That stuff's not real."

She tilted her head. She could have given him examples from Mack's experiences. But she didn't have to. "So has Braden been right? Did the fires he sensed actually happen?"

He jerked his chin, which was barely a point in his round face, up and down in a quick nod. "Yeah, but the only reasonable explanation is that he's the one setting the fires."

She understood his logic. Of course someone could predict what would happen if he personally made certain it did. Could Braden Zimmer be setting fire to the territory he'd been assigned to protect? Could he be the one putting his own team in danger?

She glanced across the room and met his gaze. He hadn't stopped staring at her since he'd sat down at the booth. The men he'd joined kept glancing her way, too—probably wondering what was drawing his attention.

What had? Was he concerned because he'd unintentionally struck her? Or because he was worried she might discover who was really responsible for setting the fires in Northern Lakes?

BRADEN'S STOMACH TWISTED into knots of apprehension. He'd been such an idiot to let Marty get to him. Not only had he hurt Sam, but he'd also left her alone with that blowhard. Gingrich thought the worst of Braden and his team and was determined to make certain everyone else did, too. Unfortunately he might succeed in convincing Sam McRooney.

With the way she was staring across the room at him—speculatively—she might have been considering what the trooper was saying. She might have begun to wonder if it was possible Braden or one of his team members was responsible for setting the fires.

She wasn't the only one being forced to listen to an idiot, though.

"You've been out of the dating pool a long time," Cody Mallehan was saying to him. "So let me explain to you how this works. When you think a woman you see in a bar is hot, you're supposed to send her a drink—not an ice pack."

A grin tugged at Braden's mouth. Cody was an idiot only because he got so much enjoyment out of giving everyone else a hard time. Other than that he was one of the best Hotshots Braden had on his team. He would trust the younger man with his life.

But he'd never previously trusted his dating advice, despite Cody's womanizing reputation—or more accurately, because of it. Things were different now, though;

Cody had recently fallen, and fallen hard, for a sweet woman. So Braden might have been tempted to listen if he had any intention of dating Sam McRooney. But he had no such intention—with her or anyone else.

"I'm not trying to pick her up," Braden said. "I accidentally hit her earlier."

A breath whistled out between Cody's teeth. "Man, you really have been out of the dating pool a long time—since the caveman times—if you think you can club a woman and drag her off. Sounds like something Ethan would do."

Ethan Sommerly glanced across the table at Cody and glared. With his bushy black beard and long hair, he did look a bit like a caveman.

Owen James followed Braden's gaze. "Her left cheek is swollen," the EMT said, assessing her condition even from across the room. He was a Hotshot, but when they were back at home base in Northern Lakes, he was also a paramedic.

Braden's stomach lurched with guilt and regret. "I accidentally caught her with my elbow."

"She's not pressing charges, is she?" Trent Miles asked. "Why's she talking to *Gingrich*?" He grimaced with disgust. During the off-season, Trent worked out of a firehouse in Detroit. He worked closely with law enforcement in the city since a lot of the fires set there were arson, so he had a healthy respect for officers. Real officers. He'd made it no secret he didn't consider Marty a real officer.

"She's not going to press charges." At least that was what she'd told him. Marty might have convinced her otherwise, though. "She's talking to him about the arson investigation."

"Why?" Cody asked. "If she knows something, she

should be talking to you." He'd apparently assumed Sam was a witness with information. "He has no business investigating the fires. He's gotten nowhere."

"Neither have I," Braden admitted. "That's why I called the chief's office. The woman talking to Gingrich is an arson investigator with the US Forest Service."

Cody leaned back in the booth and uttered a ragged sigh. "Good. We should have already stopped this son of a bitch..." Then his girlfriend wouldn't have recently lost her home and very nearly her life.

"Yes, we should have," Braden agreed. Guilt overwhelmed him again. He pushed the beer Owen had poured for him across the table. He hadn't taken a sip and had no interest in it. His stomach already felt queasy enough.

"Is that why you called the meeting for tomorrow?" Trent asked. They'd been back only a couple of days from fighting a blaze out west. Usually they had more downtime than that between assignments, so he'd been smart to conclude Braden had called the team together for another reason.

Braden nodded. "I was going to wait until the meeting tomorrow to share this. But..."

"What?" Dawson Hess asked. The assistant superintendent had just returned to the booth from the pool game he'd been shooting at the tables nearby with Braden's other assistant superintendent, Wyatt Andrews.

Braden dragged in a deep breath before admitting, "I received a note..."

Dawson tensed. "From the arsonist?"

Braden nodded. "Left on my desk in the firehouse..."

Cody cursed.

"You need to be careful," Wyatt said, his blue eyes darkening with concern.

"That's why I called the US Forest Service," Braden told his assistants. He probably should have called Wyatt and Dawson when he got the note, but Wyatt was planning a wedding, and Dawson had taken a quick trip to New York to see his girlfriend. Braden pointed across the room. "And why she's here. Her name's Sam McRooney."

"Any relation to Mack?" Cody asked.

"Daughter," Braden confirmed.

"Mack never mentioned having a daughter."

"Nobody mentions their daughters to you," Wyatt razzed him, then turned back to Braden. "I don't get why she's talking to Gingrich, though. You know way more about the arson investigation than he does."

"She called him in to protect me," Braden said. He glanced across the room again. He would have preferred her protecting him; then she'd have to stick close—real close. But then she would be in danger, too. It was better she—and everyone else—stay away from him now that he'd become the arsonist's next target.

Owen snorted. "Who's going to protect you from him? That guy has always hated you."

Thinking of Gingrich's accusation, Braden's temper flared again. "Marty's the one who needed protecting from me," he admitted. "I was about to hit him when I clipped Sam with my elbow."

Owen nodded. "Of course... Too bad she got in the way." He was a little younger than Braden and Gingrich, but he'd grown up in Northern Lakes, too. He knew the trooper too well.

Trent sighed. "Good thing she stopped you, or we'd be bailing you out of jail right now."

"At least he would've been safe in there," Dawson remarked. "Sam McRooney was right to call in protection for you. She just called the wrong person."

"I don't need a state trooper," Braden said. The last thing he wanted was anyone following him around; it was bad enough when Stanley brought Annie to the firehouse and she shadowed his every move.

"No, you don't," Owen agreed. "Not when you've got us. We'll each take a shift."

Braden shook his head. "I don't need a babysitter."

"No," Ethan Sommerly agreed. The Hotshot was the biggest loner on the team. He spent most of his time as a ranger in the middle of a national forest in the Upper Peninsula. Of course he would understand. But then he added, "You need a bodyguard."

Wyatt nodded in agreement. "If you don't want one of us, I can see if Matt can get time off from the assisted-living center to protect you."

Matt was Wyatt's soon to be brother-in-law. The kid had wanted to be a Hotshot. But when he, like hundreds of other applicants, hadn't gotten the open position as a US Forest Service firefighter, he'd decided to go back to school to become a registered nurse.

"I don't need a bodyguard, either," Braden said. He'd argued enough for the day, so he stood up. "What I need is a good night's sleep before the meeting tomorrow." He worried that might be hard, though he wasn't sure what would keep him awake longer—that note, or his guilt over accidentally hitting Sam.

Or would it be other thoughts of Sam that kept him up? She was damn beautiful.

"Braden, you can't just take off," Cody protested as he started away from the booth. "You never know when or how he might strike at you."

"I'll be vigilant," he promised his guys. "He won't sneak up on me."

From the skepticism on their faces, it was clear he

hadn't convinced them. So he added an order, "Nobody follow me. I'm perfectly safe."

He wasn't. And they knew it. But being around him would put them in danger, too. They'd already been through enough of that. He'd nearly lost Wyatt, Dawson and Cody in fires.

And Owen…

He glanced at the jagged scar on the man's cheek. He'd nearly lost the Marine on his last deployment. They all risked their lives enough doing their jobs. He wouldn't ask them to put themselves further at risk because of him. He glanced over at Sam McRooney. And he certainly wouldn't put her in danger, either.

"I can take care of myself," he assured them, and headed out of the bar before they could argue.

He appreciated and understood their concern, though. As he stepped outside, he felt an odd sensation—like he was being watched. None of them had followed him from the bar, so it had to be someone who was already outside—maybe even waiting for him? He peered around in the dark but couldn't see anyone lurking in the shadows beyond the small circles the street lamps cast on the sidewalk.

That didn't matter; he didn't need to see the person to know he was there.

Braden could've gone back inside, but he didn't. That wasn't how he wanted to live his life—in fear. He felt the shadow following as he walked the two blocks to the small home he'd rented because of its close vicinity to the firehouse. He'd had a bigger house before the divorce— one farther from town with a big yard and a lot of bedrooms. He'd intended to raise his family there.

But maybe it was good that had never happened. Because then they'd be in danger, too. Fortunately his parents had moved away from Northern Lakes a couple of years ago, to be closer to his sister and her kids. They'd promised when he gave them grandkids, they'd come home. But they were safer in Arizona—even with wildfires burning nearby. At least nature had caused those— a lightning strike—not a maniac with a match.

Whoever was following seemed to tail Braden all the way home. The skin between his shoulder blades tingled at the feeling of being watched. It hadn't made him walk any faster, though. He wasn't afraid. He was pissed. So pissed he stomped across his porch with such force his front door creaked open before he even reached for the knob. He must've left it unlocked. But he knew he'd shut it tightly; he always did.

Someone had been inside his house; undoubtedly the same person who'd been in his office earlier. He wished momentarily for the gun he kept behind the seat of his US Forest Service pickup. The shotgun was for protection from bears, though. Not people.

But while Braden suspected someone had been inside his house, he doubted he was still there. *He* was behind Braden—watching him—probably for his reaction to whatever he'd been doing inside Braden's house. Whatever he'd left behind for Braden to discover...

He stepped closer and opened the door the rest of the way. The house was dark inside; he couldn't see anything.

But he could smell it. Gasoline.

5

SAM STARED AT the closed door of the Filling Station in disbelief that Braden had just walked out without talking to her again. Not that she felt personally slighted, but professionally he'd ignored her recommendation to have someone protecting him. Of course she couldn't blame him for not trusting Gingrich to do the job.

The trooper's phone vibrated seconds before a tune pealed out—something that sounded peculiarly like something you might hear at a strip club. As Martin pulled his phone from his pocket, his wedding ring glinted in the light dangling over their table. She doubted he would have assigned that song as his wife's ringtone. But then she didn't know much about marriage beyond what a few married friends had told her. She certainly hadn't grown up with an example of it since she couldn't even remember her mom.

Gingrich didn't accept the call immediately—just stared down at his phone, his face flushing red again. "I need to take this."

"Go ahead," she said, curious about who'd put that look on his face—a mixture of shame and excitement.

"I—I won't be able to hear in here," he said. "So I'm going to take it outside. I may have to leave."

"I asked you here to discuss protection duty for Superintendent Zimmer," she reminded him.

"And I told you he's not the one who needs protecting." There was something in his voice—something almost threatening—that had Sam's patience close to snapping.

She picked up her ice pack and held it in a tight fist—more tempted to throw it at him than use it. "You're not in charge of this investigation, Trooper Gingrich," she informed him. "I am."

His face flushed an even deeper red. "But Braden doesn't want my protection any more than I want to protect him." He glanced at the table of Hotshots, then at the closed door. "He doesn't seem to understand you're in charge, either."

Though Braden had claimed he wasn't a chauvinist, she wondered if that was the case.

"I need to leave," Gingrich said as he stood. His phone began to ring again, and he hurried toward that door.

"Dick," she muttered after him.

A deep chuckle followed her remark. But she wasn't sure which of the Hotshots who suddenly surrounded her table was behind it.

"You're obviously as good a judge of character as your dad," a blond-haired firefighter remarked as he extended his hand to her. "I'm Cody Mallehan."

She shook his hand—firmly—like her father had taught her when she was just a little girl. Unfortunately she'd never gotten much bigger. She hadn't been able to excel at the things her brothers had. So she had to excel at what she could—catching arsonists.

"Mack's mentioned you," she said. "He's not too happy you didn't join him at Northern Cascades."

"That's cool of him, but I'm happy here," Cody said. "My team is my family." He introduced the other men. Wyatt Andrews and Dawson Hess. Trent Miles.

She recognized all the names. She had the roster of the entire team.

"Owen James and Ethan Sommerly left a little while ago. Owen had an EMT call and Ethan can only handle being social for so long," Cody remarked. "Otherwise, you could have met them, too."

"I do need to meet the entire team at some point," Sam said. Because, like Gingrich, she suspected one of them could be the arsonist. She'd already started investigating them. Owen James carried physical scars from war. Did he have psychological ones that could cause him to start fires?

And Sommerly was notoriously antisocial. Enough to want to hurt people?

"You'll meet everyone tomorrow," Superintendent Andrews said, "at the team meeting Braden has called."

He hadn't mentioned the meeting to her. He certainly hadn't invited her. But she didn't betray her surprise—just nodded in agreement.

"I hope you didn't believe any of that nonsense Gingrich spewed about Braden," Cody said as he settled onto the chair across from her.

"He's just jealous," Wyatt added as he turned a chair around and straddled it. "Goes back to high school and all the girls chasing after Braden instead of him."

"Braden needs some women chasing after him now," Cody remarked.

Sam's pulse quickened as she remembered how he'd looked in just that towel with water droplets trailing over his impressive chest and abs. She couldn't believe he didn't have women chasing after him now. If not for the investigation, she might be tempted to be one of those women.

Cody continued, "After what his ex-wife did to him…"

It would be her business only if it had something to do with the investigation. But then it was hard to know the arsonist's motive unless she learned everything about his latest target: Braden. So Sam asked, "What was that?"

"Cheated on him, then invited him to her wedding to the other guy," Wyatt replied. "Braden did have a couple women after him a few months ago. They mistook him for a stripper and nearly ripped off his clothes."

Sam could hardly blame them. He looked better without clothes. Not that he hadn't looked damn good in the Hotshots' casual uniform of black T-shirt and khaki cargo pants. Their official uniform while firefighting was all yellow—shirt, pants, coat and hat—so they were easier to see through the smoke and flames.

"Now the arsonist is after him," Dawson said, "and that's not good…"

"No," Sam agreed. "Especially when he refuses police protection."

Wyatt snorted. "You can't call *Marty* police protection. He's an idiot, just like you said. How the hell can he blame Braden for starting the fires?"

"Every time one of them has started we've been with him," Cody said.

Sam looked at the men gathered in a circle around her table and asked, "All of you?"

"The three of us who are based out of Northern Lakes during the off-season." Cody gestured at himself and the two assistant superintendents. "We were definitely together when that first fire started and the last one, too."

"So the four of you were together?" she asked. One person might lie for another, might even be working with another—although that was rare for arsonists unless they were hired to start fires for insurance claims. But four?

Cody groaned. "You let Gingrich get to you."

She shook her head. She'd had her suspicions before she'd even talked to the state trooper. And while the four of them could alibi one another, that left sixteen other Hotshot suspects. "You're very protective of your boss," she remarked, "yet you all just let him walk out of here alone." She included herself in that accusation. Her heart shifted again, contracting with a spasm of fear. Was he all right?

"He gave us direct orders *not* to follow him," Wyatt said.

"And, what? You've never disobeyed one of his direct orders before?" she asked. She'd read the report on the first fire. She knew Wyatt Andrews had refused Braden's command to return to base. He'd refused to leave the fire until he'd located the missing campers. Her gaze swung toward Dawson Hess and Cody Mallehan. Against Braden's orders, they had returned to the fire to help Wyatt.

"You're definitely Mack's daughter," Cody remarked.

She narrowed her eyes. "Is that a compliment?" She wasn't certain. Mack wasn't always the easiest person—especially with her.

He grinned. "Definitely a compliment."

"Careful," Wyatt warned him. "You're nearly engaged. You can't be complimenting other women anymore."

"I just meant she knows her stuff," Cody said. Then he turned back toward her. "You're thorough."

"That's how I close cases," she said. "I know how to do my job." Had they come over here to question her abilities? She was used to being underestimated—especially by alpha males like them. But she suspected they had another motive, particularly when she noticed Dawson Hess studying her face.

When he realized she'd caught him staring, he pointed toward her cheek. "You should have used the ice pack Braden sent over," he advised. "It would have stopped the swelling and minimized the bruising."

Makeup would minimize the bruising, too. She shrugged off his concern. "It's fine."

"You know Braden feels horrible about that," Cody said. "He would never hurt a woman."

"I know," she said. "I didn't press charges—no matter how much Gingrich tried to convince me otherwise." Calling him to protect Braden was a mistake she wouldn't repeat. But could his team be trusted to protect him?

Only Wyatt, Cody and Dawson, who'd been together when the fires had started. If that was true, none of them could be the arsonist. But what about the sixteen other members of the team?

Did they have alibis? Because the fires only happened when the Hotshots were in town, it was entirely possible the arsonist was one of them—which put Braden in more danger. He was unlikely to suspect one of his own.

She needed to talk to him—needed to make him aware of the threat. He wouldn't want to hear it, of course, any more than her dad would want to hear that one of *his* team members couldn't be trusted. Plus, it was late—felt even later since she'd traveled all day. She had yet to check into her hotel. And apparently she'd have to get up early to crash the Hotshot meeting Braden had called.

But she knew she wouldn't be able to sleep until she'd made certain he was safe. "Where does Braden live?" she asked.

"Are you going to protect him?" Cody asked.

She could. She had a gun, and she knew how to use it.

But knowledge might keep him safer than her weapon. Still, he wouldn't be cautious if he couldn't accept that the arsonist might be someone close to him.

"I need to talk to him," she said.

One of Cody's blond brows arched, as if he wondered if there was more to her wanting to see Braden. Sure, she was attracted to him. He was a good-looking man. But she had no intention of acting on that attraction.

All she wanted was to do her job—to catch the arsonist. But how many arsonists would she need to catch before her father started bragging about her and not just her brothers?

"I need to talk to him about the meeting," she said. And how she wanted to interrogate every member of his team after it...

Cody nodded, but there was skepticism and something else in his eyes—as if he didn't entirely believe her. Or hoped she had another reason for wanting to go to Braden's house this late at night.

Truly, she just wanted to make sure he was safe. But as she followed his men's directions down the dark street toward his house, she wondered who would make sure she was safe. Because she didn't feel safe at all. And it had nothing to do with the arsonist and everything to do with seeing Braden Zimmer again.

BRADEN'S GUTS TIGHTENED into a knot of dread. Who the hell should he call to report the arsonist being inside his house? The state police? Gingrich would probably think the gas-soaked hay bale proved Braden's guilt. And Sam...

He wasn't sure what the hell Sam would think. Had Gingrich raised her suspicions? Did she have doubts about him now? Of course the arsonist was unlikely to burn down his own damn house. Not that it had been burned down.

There was only the one small hay bale sitting inside his living room. But it had been soaked in gasoline. The odor hung heavily in the air. He'd opened the windows, and the curtains billowed in the chilly evening breeze.

Just as he'd suspected, the arsonist hadn't been waiting inside for him. He just left this message, which was even more blatant than the note. Gasoline-soaked hay bales were both his igniter and accelerant. Had he intended to start a fire in Braden's house and had been interrupted? Or was he just taunting him that he could have?

Braden suspected the latter. He needed to call Sam— once he found his phone. He must have dropped it in the living room when he tripped over the bale. After getting gasoline on his pants and all over his skin, he'd wanted to clean up before calling anyone. Even after a shower, he could still smell the gasoline on his body. He thought about stepping back under the spray, but a noise on the porch drew his attention.

He stepped out of the bathroom just as a shadow passed the front windows. He sucked in a breath. Had the son of a bitch come back with a match?

Did he intend to start the blaze now—with Braden inside? But then knuckles bumped against the wooden door. He doubted the arsonist would knock.

The breath he'd sucked in slipped out in a ragged sigh. He shouldn't have been surprised that at least one of the guys, if not all of them, would come by to check on him. Of course they would ignore his order to leave him alone. They could definitely be selective about which of his commands they followed sometimes. He'd have to bring that up at the morning meeting. But when he opened the door, he was shocked into silence because he hadn't expected *her*.

How had she even known where he lived? Sam McRooney stood on his front porch, her face washed in the golden glow from the kerosene lanterns he'd converted to porch lights. Her cheek had swollen some more and was beginning to shift from red to purple.

Guilt made him feel even queasier than the smell of gasoline had. Hitting her had been an accident, but it was an accident he could've prevented had he kept his temper in check.

He knew better than to let jerks like Marty get to him. But then he'd been on edge—not just from the arsonist but from her. Or maybe it was like the guys had told him: he needed to get laid. Hell, Cody had left a box of condoms on his desk a couple of weeks ago.

He'd forgotten all about those until now—until he'd met Sam. Now not just guilt churned his stomach. Desire did, too. Even with the bruise, she was so damn beautiful.

Her mouth gaped as she stared at him. "Do you have something against wearing clothes?"

He glanced down at the towel knotted around his hips. "I just got out of the shower."

"Again?" she asked, and her voice squeaked slightly. "You must be the cleanest guy in Northern Lakes."

"Not according to Trooper Gingrich," he said.

"He's an idiot," she said.

And Braden laughed with relief. He'd been worried Marty might have gotten to her.

She shivered—though he was the one wearing only a towel. The early autumn wind was brisk and cold, but he wasn't chilled. The wind tangled her blond hair around her face. She reached up to tug silken strands from her long black lashes.

Desire had his stomach muscles clenching. Maybe he wasn't the only one feeling the attraction, since her gaze kept slipping away from his to slide down his chest. It almost felt like a caress against his bare skin.

"Aren't you cold?" she asked.

He stepped back and gestured for her to come inside—not just to get out of the cold but to inspect what had become a crime scene. She hesitated before crossing the threshold into his living room. The small house had no foyer; the front door opened right into the living room. When he shut the door behind her, she tensed.

"It smells like gasoline in here," she said.

"Because of that," he said and gestured at the small bale—the kind someone would use for a little Halloween display—lying next to his front door. "I tripped over it when I got home—that's why I had to shower."

She bent over and examined the bale. His gaze went to her ass. It was perfectly round. His hands twitched with the urge to touch it. But he had no doubt she would hit him, and it wouldn't be an accident.

"What the hell is that doing in your living room?" she asked as she whirled back around to face him. "How did that get in here?"

He shrugged, and her gaze skimmed across his shoulders. He felt it more than the wind blowing through the curtains. "I don't know," he said. "You'd have to ask the arsonist. I don't know if I came home before he had time to light it or if this is just his way of sending me another warning."

"He's going to have to make that a little clearer for you," Sam agreed. "You seem kind of dense."

He sucked in a breath. "Good to know you don't think I'm an arsonist—just stupid."

"You are," she said, "if you don't take these threats

seriously. It's a good thing your guys told me where I could find you since you obviously had no intention of calling me about what you found here tonight, or about the meeting you're having tomorrow."

He sighed. "They're idiots…"

"Why?" she asked. "For being honest with me? For correctly assuming I should be at that meeting?"

He'd honestly forgotten all about it—once she'd arrived. She'd distracted him right away. "I intended to tell you about the meeting. And I was going to call you about this—" his hand shook as he gestured at the bale "—as soon as I washed the gasoline off."

She sucked in a breath. "That makes sense—if he came back and you had any gasoline on you…" She shuddered. "But you still should've called me right away. What if he's still hanging around…"

Braden suspected he was—that he was watching to see how much he'd rattled him. That was another reason he hadn't immediately called anyone. He didn't want to let the guy think he was getting to him. He shrugged. "I didn't see anyone…"

But he had felt another presence.

"I'll call the state police," she said as she reached for her phone. "Have them canvass the area."

He caught her hand before she could press any buttons. "Not Gingrich…"

"I won't make that mistake again," she said as she touched her fingers to her bruise.

His stomach lurched, and he reached out, following the path her fingers had taken over the swollen cheekbone. "I'm so sorry."

"I know," she said. "You told me a few times. It's fine. I know better than to get in the middle of a fight."

"I shouldn't have let Marty get to me."

"No, you shouldn't have," she agreed. "I understand why you don't want him protecting you. But you should have let one of the guys come home with you."

"I'm surprised they didn't come anyway," he admitted. Instead they'd let her come. His eyes narrowed with suspicion.

"What?" she asked. "Are you wondering if one of them had something to do with this?" She gestured at the bale again.

He gasped with shock that she'd suspect one of his team members. Marty *had* gotten to her. "Hell, no. They're not arsonists. But they might be nearly as bad."

"What's that supposed to mean?" she asked. "What are they? Murderers?"

Heat rushed to his face, but he had to tell her now, even though it was embarrassing. "Matchmakers," he admitted.

She laughed, but it sounded a bit nervous. "No..."

He ran his fingers through his still-damp hair. "Ever since my divorce, they've been trying to set me up with someone—anyone, really."

"I'm anyone?"

"You're female," he said. "And damn good-looking." He hadn't meant to say that, too; he didn't want it to be awkward between them.

But she must have heard the compliment so many times before that she didn't react except for a slight blush.

"I thought sex didn't matter to you," she said, throwing his earlier words back at him.

He groaned. "I hope you didn't tell them I said that..."

She shook her head. "Your secret is safe with me."

"You talked to my guys," he said with a heavy sigh of resignation. "I'm sure I have no secrets anymore."

"Your secrets are definitely not safe with them," she agreed.

So they'd told her what a fool he'd been. More heat rushed to his face. She touched it like he'd touched hers, skimming her fingertips across his cheek.

"I'm sorry," she said, "about your ex-wife."

"She didn't sleep with you, too, did she?" he asked.

She laughed. "No. Sex does matter to me."

And now the heat rushed lower in his body. He'd thought it hadn't mattered. But he suddenly realized how long it had been since he'd been this attracted to a woman.

Hell, maybe he'd never been this attracted to a woman.

He hoped she didn't look down, because his damp towel was about to give away just how attracted he was. As if she'd read his mind, she lowered her gaze, and her breath escaped in a soft gasp.

She shook her head, but didn't step back when he moved closer. She just raised her gaze to his and murmured, "This is a bad idea."

He couldn't argue with her, not with the smell of gasoline burning in his nose. It was crazy to get involved with anyone now—it would only put that person in danger. "I know," he agreed. "But for the first time I think I understand the arsonist…"

Her brow furrowed as she stared up at him. "How?"

"I understand how sometimes you just have a compulsion to do something and you can't fight it…" That was how he'd heard some arsonists describe the urge to set fires—an unquenchable thirst. Until now he'd never had such a compelling desire to do something he knew was a mistake.

Until now he'd never had such a compelling desire at all…

"You feel a compulsion to set a fire?" she asked.

"I feel a compulsion to do this..." He touched her—just his fingertips along her jaw. Her skin was so silky, just like her hair, which brushed across his hand. He tipped up her chin and lowered his head to hers. When their mouths touched, he felt a jolt. Maybe it should've brought him to his senses. But that compulsion overwhelmed him. He skimmed his lips across hers. They were so soft.

Maybe she felt that jolt, too, because she gasped. And he deepened the kiss, dipping his tongue inside her mouth to taste her. She was sweet and sexy and hot.

Her hands moved between their bodies. But instead of pushing him back, they skimmed over his bare chest. His heart leaped against her palm—beating harder and faster as desire rushed over him like the wind blowing through the open window.

He felt the fire burning between them.

Then something besides the breeze blew through the open window—dropping onto the hardwood floor with a crash of breaking glass. Air whooshed—not from the window, but from the explosion of the burning rag catching the gasoline fumes on fire. Someone had tossed a Molotov cocktail inside, and now there was a real fire burning in the house. And like his kissing Sam, it was immediately out of control.

6

FIRE FLASHED AS the flames inside the broken bottle spread across the hardwood floor. The small hay bale ignited in a shower of burning embers. Heat penetrated Sam's jeans, threatening to scorch her skin. The sensation instantly made her concerned for Braden, who wore only a towel.

But instead of jumping back, he lifted her up, or at least he tried. She struggled in his arms. He didn't need to carry her to safety.

"Put me down and get me a damn extinguisher!" she yelled over the rush of fire consuming the curtains and running up the walls.

Maybe it was too late for an extinguisher. She reached for the blanket on the back of the couch. But before she could whip it at the flames, they attacked the wool. She dropped it before it burned her hands. The flames spread from the blanket to the couch, climbing up the back of it. The fire was behind her and in front of her—circling around her, nearly trapping her. But she could still get out the front door. She moved toward it, dodging the flames as they began to close around her.

Maybe Braden had been smart in trying to carry her

away. Where had he gone? Was he all right? She hesitated before reaching the front door. Should she look for him?

Mercifully, she didn't have to as he rushed back in from the other side of the couch. But instead of grabbing her again, he thrust an extinguisher at her. This was no under-the-counter kitchen model. It was a heavy, industrial-sized can.

She pulled open the canister and directed it at the flames. She started at the top, where the flames had climbed the curtains to lap at the ceiling. If that caught, the roof might collapse in on them. But with the flames consuming the gasoline-soaked hardwood, the floor could also collapse beneath them.

Before she could direct her extinguisher there, water sprayed across the flames. Wyatt appeared, dragging a garden hose into the house. They worked together, fighting the fire. But the gasoline had spread farther across the floor than they'd realized.

The arsonist had set the stage for a conflagration. Despite how hard they fought, the flames continued to spread. "We have to get out," Braden yelled at her.

But it wasn't just the roar of the fire he had to yell over, it was the wailing of sirens, too. The front door burst open as firefighters in full gear rushed into the house. Even through their face masks, Sam could see the fear in their eyes.

Cody rushed forward and pulled Sam toward the door while Wyatt caught Braden's arm and dragged him out. As they exited, more firefighters rushed inside, lugging the high pressure hose. They turned the nozzle and the water gushed out, dousing the flames far more easily than the garden hose and extinguisher had.

Sam sputtered for breath as tears flowed from her burning eyes. Caught up in the moment—in the fight with the fire—she hadn't noticed the smoke or the heat. But she noticed it now. She just wasn't certain which moment had distracted her more—the fire or the kiss.

"You need oxygen," Dawson told her as he pushed a mask against her face.

She sucked in a breath of pure air, and it was as much a shock to her system as Braden's kiss had been. She'd never felt anything like that instant reaction. There had been no moment of awkwardness—no self-consciousness, no trying to align noses or lips. They'd just fit.

And it had been hot even before the fire had started.

She coughed and sputtered and pawed at the mask until Dawson pulled it away. "As soon as Owen shows up, I'll have him take you to the hospital to get checked out." He pointed at his boss. "You, too!"

Braden didn't even glance at him; he just stared at his house. The fire hose extinguished the flames, but smoke continued to pour from the open windows and roof. Was it out or only coiling back to strike again? Some fires were like that—like snakes.

Remembering the difficult blazes she'd fought, she shuddered. Dawson, who occasionally worked as an EMT like Owen James, wrapped a blanket around her shoulders. She wasn't the one who needed that.

Braden still wore only his towel, which had slipped so low his hip bones jutted out above it. Now the wind tugged at the terry cloth. While she wouldn't necessarily mind if he lost the towel, she didn't want him to be embarrassed later. So she shrugged off the blanket and draped it around him.

"I'm fine," Sam assured Dawson. "I don't need to go to the hospital." But she did need to know where Owen James was. On another call? Or was he the one who'd thrown the bottle into the window and hadn't had time to get back to the firehouse yet? And what of Trent Miles or Ethan Sommerly? She didn't see them, either.

"But you could have lung damage from smoke inhalation—"

"I was a firefighter before I became an arson investigator," she said. "I would know if I do."

What about Braden? Was he all right? He had refused the oxygen. Well, he actually hadn't refused it; he'd just completely ignored it.

"Braden?" she called to him.

But he didn't hear her—his focus was on the two guys walking out of his house.

"It's out," Cody said after pulling off his hat and mask. "And the damage is confined to the living room."

Braden glanced at her then. "Because of Sam…"

She shook her head. "I didn't fight it alone." They had fought back the flames as a team.

Cody shook his head. "You're both damn fools," he said. "You didn't have the right gear, and the place had been doused with gasoline. You could've been killed. You should have run."

"And let him win?" Braden asked. "Not going to happen. And I'm damn well not going to let him burn down my whole house and probably half the neighborhood as well."

"We would've gotten here in time to stop that from happening," Cody said.

They had been fast. But even as fast as they'd been, the house would have been gone. And like Braden had pointed out, the fire could have spread to the adjacent homes as well.

The Hotshot superintendent shook his head. "It wasn't a risk I was willing to take."

"You did take a risk," Sam said, "when you didn't immediately report finding that gasoline-soaked hay bale inside your house."

"You found that earlier?" Wyatt asked.

Braden's head jerked in a sharp nod. "I fell over the damn thing."

Cody glanced down at his towel. "So that's why you took a shower…"

"I was covered in gasoline."

Sam shuddered to think what would have happened had he not showered. He could have gone up in flames as quickly as the hay bale had.

"You still should have called me right away," she said. "And you should have let me call in the state police…" Instead of distracting her with kisses. "If there had been patrol cars here when the arsonist returned, he wouldn't have dared throw that bottle."

Braden reminded her, "I didn't want ole Marty coming by my house."

"Marty was busy," Sam said. And now she wondered just what the hell he'd been busy doing—getting ready to throw a bottle? "They would have sent someone else."

"I didn't need someone else," he said. "You were there."

She hadn't been much protection. The arsonist had thrown the bottle, anyway. Maybe he'd even thrown it *because* she was there.

Had he been outside, watching them as they'd kissed? Had he waited until that precise moment to throw the bottle with the burning rag inside it?

The guys turned toward her. "Did you see anything?"

She shook her head. "No." But she'd been distracted.

"Did you?" Dawson asked Braden—who just shook his head.

She tensed, waiting for them to ask why they hadn't seen anything—to ask what they'd been doing. And her face heated more than it had during the fire. Of course during the fire, she hadn't felt anything. She'd focused only on putting out those flames. And then afterward, on putting that kiss out of her mind.

"We're fine," Braden said. "We didn't get hurt. You guys don't need to worry."

Cody stepped closer to his boss and said, "I know you have this thing where you feel responsible for everything and everyone, like you gotta take care of them. But you got to take care of yourself, too."

Sam blinked. Maybe it was just the smoke still tearing up her eyes, or maybe it was seeing how much Braden's men respected and loved him. No wonder her dad liked Braden so much; the two were a lot alike. Too damn much alike for her.

Her entire life she'd had to fight her father to stop being so protective, to stop treating her like she wasn't as strong and capable as her brothers. She didn't want to have to fight a man just like Mack—not that she had considered a future with Braden.

As incredible as it had been, it had been just a kiss. She wouldn't risk another—wouldn't risk it distracting her from the job she loved.

BRADEN BRACED HIMSELF before picking up the phone. He hadn't expected this call so soon. But he had figured it would come eventually and had been dreading it. He lifted the receiver but hesitated before he pressed the blinking button on the handset in his office.

He'd lost his cell phone in the fire. It must have dropped out of his pocket when he'd fallen over the gasoline-soaked hay bale. It had probably burned up with the couch and everything else he'd had in the small living room.

While the fire had been contained to that room, smoke had damaged the rest of the house, making it uninhabitable. The few hours he'd slept the night before had been on a cot in the firehouse.

He drew in a deep breath and pushed the blinking button. "Hey, Mack…"

"What took you so long to pick up?" the smoke jumper leader asked, but he sounded more anxious than impatient. "Everything okay?"

"You know it's not or you wouldn't be calling," Braden said.

The older man uttered a loud laugh that sounded more like a bark. "Busted."

"Did Sam call you?" he wondered.

Just how close were she and her father? What had she shared with him? Information about the fire or about the kiss before it? Or maybe about his accidentally hitting her. No. If she'd told Mack that, the smoke jumper leader probably wouldn't be calling; he would have flown to Northern Lakes to kick Braden's butt.

"If Sam had called me, I would be talking to her," Mack pointed out. "Not you."

"So how did you…?" He didn't wait for Mack to answer before he shouted his own reply, "Cody!" Damn him and his big mouth.

"I won't reveal my source," Mack said.

"You're not a reporter. So that excuse doesn't work for you."

"Do you want to argue or tell me what the hell happened?"

"Didn't your *source* tell you?" Fortunately Cody didn't know about the kiss, so he couldn't have shared that.

Mack cursed him. "Why aren't you willing to talk?"

Braden laughed. "I could say the same. You never told me you had a daughter."

"There's a reason for that."

Probably because she was beautiful and he didn't want every guy he knew hitting on her.

"Sometimes guys in leadership positions make enemies," Mack continued. "And I wouldn't want someone using my daughter to get back at me."

"Everybody knows about your sons," Braden pointed out.

"Maybe I wouldn't care if someone took on one of them." Mack laughed. "They can take care of themselves."

Despite his exhaustion, Braden sat up straighter in his chair as he got defensive. "And you don't think Sam can?"

Mack sure as hell didn't know his daughter very well.

"She believes she can," her father said. "But she's not as tough as she thinks she is."

She was strong. But she wasn't tough—at least, not physically. She was soft with generous curves and silky hair and skin. He might have slept better upon returning to the firehouse last night if he hadn't kept thinking of her—and that kiss. Every time he'd closed his eyes, he hadn't seen those flames. He'd seen her face, tipped up toward his as he'd kissed her. And desire had overwhelmed him…

"I know about the fire last night," Mack admitted. "I know she was in it."

"She put it out," Braden said. "She must have been a hell of a firefighter."

"She was," Mack agreed. "But she works too hard—takes too many risks—to prove she's as tough as her brothers."

Braden suspected it wasn't her brothers she was trying to prove anything to. It was her father. "I'm sure she is," Braden said.

"She's going to get herself killed if she keeps taking risks..."

Getting involved with Braden would be the greatest risk Sam could take. That could prove the most dangerous thing she'd ever done. It had nearly gotten her burned last night. He had to make certain nobody thought they were involved—especially him.

Maybe his guys were right that he needed to start dating again. But he needed to date a woman who lived in Northern Lakes, not one who was only there short term to do a job. His life was here—his job, his team...

"Maybe she wouldn't do that as much," Braden said, "if everyone knew she was your daughter?" Because most people feared the bald-headed smoke jumper base leader. "Don't you think that would protect her more?"

Mack sighed. "That might protect her. But not me. She doesn't want me interfering in her life."

She was proud. And stubborn. Like her father.

A grin tugged at Braden's lips. "Is that what this call is?" he teased. "You not interfering?"

"Well, she's not going to find out about this call, right?" Mack prodded him.

Braden didn't want to get in the middle of family drama. He took enough calls from his sister complaining about their parents overstepping with her kids. During every one of those calls, she'd begged him to start having kids so their folks would move home to Northern Lakes. At least the divorce had stopped Heather from urging him to procreate.

Not that he didn't want a family of his own someday. He wanted that very much—to be a father, to coach sports and watch dance recitals. He wanted to be the kind of parent his parents had been, loving and supportive.

"No, she won't find out from…" Braden trailed off as Sam pushed open his office door and walked around his desk.

She snatched the phone from his hand, her fingers brushing over his. His skin tingled in reaction, but she didn't even glance at him. She was focused on the call, so focused that she settled onto the edge of the desk next to him. Her hip bumped against the arm he'd braced on the surface.

"Hey, Mack," she said, her usually soft voice a little husky. Maybe she had inhaled more smoke than she should've the night before. Or maybe she hadn't gotten much more sleep than he had.

Before Braden could comment on it, her father must've because she replied, "I'm fine."

But she wasn't fine. Her beautiful face was tense, and her eyes were dark with anger. "This is my job," she reminded him. "You were fine with it when you asked me to look into the Northern Lakes fires."

How had she known it was her father on the phone? Stanley must have told her. The kid had answered the call before Braden had the chance.

Mack's voice was just a deep rumble; Braden couldn't make out any of what he said. But Sam's face flushed with color, highlighting the bruise on her cheek. The swelling had gone down, but the skin had a purple tint to it.

A twinge of guilt and regret struck him. He never should have let Marty get to him. Usually he wouldn't have. He was afraid his friends were right about him; he'd gone too long without sex.

Sam's arrival in Northern Lakes had made him even

more aware of that—because he was so aware of her. She sat so close to him. The heat from her body traveled from her hip against his arm straight to his groin.

He wanted her. Badly.

She uttered a ragged sigh. "Mack," she said, and now her voice softened slightly, though it was clear she was still irritated. "You don't need to worry about me."

Her father wasn't the only one worried. But Braden wasn't just worried about her getting hurt; he was worried about her hurting him. The arsonist was only part of the reason he hadn't started dating since the divorce. He hadn't wanted to risk getting hurt again.

"I am always careful," she promised her father. But she finally looked at Braden, and there was something in her gaze. Maybe regret. Maybe fear. Did she consider him as dangerous as he considered her?

"Love you, too," she said before she twisted around and hung up the receiver. Her breast bumped against Braden's shoulder as she did. She tensed. As if just realizing where she was, she scrambled off the desk in such haste her boots nearly slipped on the concrete floor.

Braden caught her, his hands naturally going for her hips. With him sitting and her standing, his face was level with her breasts, which pushed against her blue sweater.

He remembered how soft and full they'd felt against his bare chest the night before. He wanted to see them— wanted to feel them with no clothes between them. His hands contracted against her hips.

Her breath escaped in a puff. And she stared down at him like she'd looked at him earlier. Like she was a little afraid of him...

What had Mack said to her?

Everything that Braden should have said? That being around him was dangerous?

Footsteps echoed off the concrete floor and walls of the firehouse as the team arrived for the meeting. She startled and stepped back, tugging free of his grasp. But the footsteps echoed from the stairwell down the hall. They probably thought he was already in the conference room.

He stood and asked her, "Are you ready for the meeting?"

She arched a blond brow. "Are you sure you want me there?"

"I intended to invite you," he said. "You're the reason I called it."

She studied him through the thick fringe of her lashes before nodding. "Okay. But before I join, can I use your office for a phone call?" she asked.

"Of course."

He closed the door as he left to give her privacy. And he wondered who she was calling. A boyfriend?

She'd let him kiss her the night before. But from Ami he'd learned that didn't mean anything; she could already be involved with someone. As beautiful as she was, he would be more surprised if she wasn't. But that was good. He wouldn't be tempted to give in to his attraction to her—or worse yet, fall for her.

That would only put them both at risk. The fire last night had proved to him just how much danger he was in. He had to be more careful—especially around Sam McRooney. Or he might lose his heart and his life.

7

ALL EYES FOCUSED on her the moment Sam stepped into the conference room. She glanced down to make sure she had all her clothes on, shaken by memories of that recurring dream where she stood naked before a team of Hotshots. Even though she wore a blue cardigan and jeans, she felt naked standing before Braden. What had Mack said to him? What had he overheard?

Mack was so loud. Had Braden heard him cautioning her about him? *He's just gotten over a horrible divorce, Sammi. He's not ready for anything serious. So don't go falling for him. Be careful...*

How the hell had her father known she was attracted to the Hotshot superintendent? Was it just that legendary judgment of his? Or did he have guys spying on her everywhere?

When would he trust her to take care of herself?

She had assured Mack she was always careful. And she was always careful—professionally. She hadn't always been so smart in her personal life, though. Braden Zimmer—and his hard, sculpted, muscular body—made her stupider than she'd ever felt. She struggled to think around him, especially when he was wearing only a towel.

"There she is," Braden said from the far end of a long, narrow table. He stood behind a lectern while his team sat around the table. The room was so big there was also a section where chairs had been aligned in rows—four or five chairs each. "For those of you who haven't met the US Forest Service arson investigator, this is Sam McRooney."

She smiled and nodded but didn't look at him. Every time she did, her skin heated and that image of him in only a towel flashed through her mind. She couldn't be distracted now—not when she already had people questioning her qualifications.

The person questioning her most had been her own damn father. Had he really thought she would let a good-looking man distract her enough that she'd get hurt—emotionally or physically?

Of course the arsonist had literally struck during their kiss the night before. They'd been lucky they hadn't gotten burned—or worse. But that had been a coincidence...

She looked around the table until she found Cody Mallehan. He wouldn't meet her gaze, though. Mack had admitted Cody was the one who'd called her father, and not just to tell him about the fire. He'd been asking about her—about how likely she was to actually catch the arsonist. Of course Mack had wanted her to know that her abilities were already being questioned; he'd always been harder on her than anyone else.

Thanks to Mack, Sam was used to having to prove herself. She'd also grown up having to show her brothers she was just as strong and smart and capable as they were. She would show these Hotshots the same. She would catch the arsonist who'd been terrorizing and eluding them for months.

Last night the arsonist had made it as personal for her as it had been for the Huron Hotshots. She wanted this guy behind bars, but first she wanted him in front of her—she wanted to question him like the Hotshots had been questioning her.

"Do you have any suspects?" a female Hotshot asked the question.

Sam mentally ran down the roster. The woman was either Henrietta "Hank" Rowlins or Michaela Momber. A thick brown braid dangled over her shoulder and hung over the front of her black T-shirt while the other woman's blond hair was cut as short or shorter than some of the guys. "And you are?" she asked.

"Hank," the woman replied. "So do you?" She was as no-nonsense as her name.

"She's only just taken over the case," Braden said, jumping to her defense.

Just like Cody had said, Braden was quick to protect everyone else. *She* didn't need his protection, though.

"I'm working on a lead right now," she admitted. That was the call she'd made in Braden's office. But that wasn't the only lead she had.

Her other leads were right here—in this room. She knew Cody, Wyatt, Dawson and Braden had been together when most, if not all, of the fires had started. But she didn't know if the other sixteen Hotshots had alibis. She only knew that the fires had never happened when they were off fighting wildfires outside Northern Lakes. The fires were set when they were here, making it quite possible that one of them was setting the fires. But why?

"What's your lead?" Ethan Sommerly asked. Did his

deep voice hold a hint of nerves? Was he worried she was on to him?

She'd already begun checking out the bearded forest ranger as a possible suspect. He and Owen James had left the Filling Station right after Braden had. They hadn't stuck together. Owen had told the others he'd had an EMT call, which she was following up on along with her other lead. And Ethan had gone off alone, which seemed to be what he preferred.

She smiled in reply. "I'll let you know if it pans out." While she was checking out all the Hotshots, she wasn't as sure what their motives might be to set fires and especially to target Braden.

She was focusing on the person who'd already betrayed his motive—his bitter resentment of Braden. Her call hadn't gone over well. She'd offended the local state police post when she'd asked for the dash-cam footage from one of the trooper's patrol cars. In order to get the sergeant to send it, she would probably have to have the US Forest Service chief give him a call from Washington. Maybe then he would understand how serious this was.

She and Braden could have been killed last night. The thought bothered her, but so did the question of what might have happened if the arsonist hadn't interrupted their kiss. Where would it have led? To Braden's bedroom?

If they'd been in bed when the burning bottle was tossed through the window, they might not have had time to escape, let alone fight the fire.

She shuddered. Not just at the thought of what could have happened because of the fire, but what could have happened had they made it to a bed...

His towel hadn't left much to her imagination. She had a pretty good idea of how impressive he was. Heat rushed to her face, and she forced herself to focus on all the possible suspects in the room with her now.

She'd met Wyatt, Dawson, Cody and Trent. In checking out Owen and Ethan, she knew what they looked like. Now she knew who Hank was, and by process of elimination, Michaela, too. But she wasn't certain about the others.

Could one of them have thrown that bottle? Could any of them resent Braden or the team enough to want to hurt them?

They seemed to all get along with a warm, friendly camaraderie, and a respect and affection for their superintendent. She hoped it wasn't one of them. She hoped more for Braden's sake than any of theirs. He'd already been betrayed, in the worst possible way, when his wife had cheated on him. It would be too much if somone on his team had betrayed him as well.

DESPITE NOT HAVING much sleep, Braden wasn't tired. He had an almost nervous energy—a restlessness—that wouldn't let him relax. He was too edgy.

So he adjusted his grip on the barbell and raised it over his head. His arms strained with the weight, but he welcomed the challenge. One rep. Two. Three...

He punished his body, lifting over and over, but the tension didn't ease. He couldn't exhaust himself—no matter how much he tried. He had just snapped the barbell back into the holder when he noticed the shadow stretching across the concrete floor.

His sweat-damp skin chilled, and he shivered with fear. Not of the arsonist, but of Sam McRooney. He recognized that curvy, nearly hourglass shadow.

"I'm sorry," she said. "I thought you went to the Filling Station with the rest of your team."

The meeting had gone late, with everyone sharing what they'd seen and heard at every fire. He was pretty sure it had been a waste of Sam's time since everything they'd told her she'd probably already read in the reports. But she hadn't just listened; she'd asked questions, too.

Gingrich might not have been able to convince her of Braden's guilt. But he'd made her doubt the rest of his team. She'd just about interrogated every member except for Cody, Wyatt and Dawson. She must have known from the reports that they could provide an alibi for each other. "No," he said. He'd wanted to clear his mind, not cloud it. But the reason he was distracted stood before him right now in shorts and a tank top.

"My motel doesn't have a gym," she said. "And I felt like working out."

Was she edgy, too? He doubted it was because she hadn't had sex in a while. Along with her beauty, she had a sensuality about her. It was blatant right now in those short shorts and that tight tank top.

He swallowed a groan as desire overwhelmed him. He was glad his shorts were loose. But he turned slightly away from her as he picked up a towel and mopped the sweat off his face.

"Were you leaving?" she asked.

He wasn't sure if she sounded hopeful or disappointed. He shook his head. "Thanks to the arsonist I don't have any place to go," he reminded her. "I'll be staying here until my house is habitable again."

"I'm sorry," she said again.

"You helped put it out," he said. "It could have been worse."

She shuddered. "It could have been." She reached out and squeezed his forearm, and his skin tingled beneath her fingertips. "I will find the arsonist."

He'd had a woman make him promises before. She'd taught him how easily promises could be made when the person had no intention of keeping them. But Sam seemed earnest, like she didn't make them lightly.

Still, he really didn't know her. He knew her father, but it was obvious they weren't close. Why not? Did she remind him too much of his wife?

"You can trust me," she said, as if she'd realized his struggle to do just that.

A grin tugged up the corners of his mouth. "That's not easy for me to do anymore."

She nodded. "I understand. I haven't always made the smartest choices, either."

"Men?"

She grinned. "Yes. Again, sex does matter to me."

"You're not going to let me live that down," he said.

"I have brothers," she said. "They never let me live anything down…"

"Any other men in your life right now?" he asked. Damn, Cody. He was right. Braden had been out of the dating pool so long that he was rusty. He felt awkward just asking that. How would he ever ask someone out?

Not that he had any intention of asking out Sam. The way she stared at him for several long moments made him feel even more uncomfortable. Like she wondered why he was asking.

Then because she was straightforward, she did ask, "Why?"

"You let me kiss you last night," he said.

"And you want to know if I would have done that if I was seeing someone else?"

He did want to know that, but he realized now it was none of his business. "I'm sorry," he said. "That was out of line."

Their relationship was professional, not personal. That kiss never should've happened.

"And the kiss wasn't?" she asked.

He sighed. "I didn't have time to apologize for that," he reminded her. They'd been a little busy trying to put out a fire.

She tilted her head, and her hair brushed across the bruise on her cheek. Maybe she was still waiting for that apology.

He owed her one. She'd already thought he was a chauvinist. Hitting on her had probably only reinforced that opinion. But more than an apology, he owed it to her to keep her safe. He'd also promised her father that, and Braden didn't make promises he didn't fully intend to keep. The best way for him to protect her would be to keep a safe distance, so nobody would make the mistake of thinking they meant anything to each other personally.

But he'd never felt like this before—never been so attracted, so infatuated. "It would be a waste of time for me to apologize now..."

"Why is that?" she asked.

"Because we both know that if you're not seeing anyone right now, I'll probably do it again."

She sighed. "Well, I'm not seeing anyone. So you probably will..."

He wrapped one end of his towel around one hand, then linked it behind her back. Pulling on the other end, he propelled her forward until she stumbled against his body.

She lifted her hands and braced them against his chest. It was bare again. Knowing he was alone in the firehouse, he hadn't bothered with a shirt.

But he hadn't been alone. At least not for long. How

had she gotten inside? He'd told Stanley to lock the door when he'd left. Damn kid...

Hopefully she'd locked that door—because this time, Braden didn't want to be interrupted. He lowered his head and kissed her. He felt that same immediate jolt of desire so intense it flowed throughout his body, making him tingle everywhere.

She moved her lips across his, sliding them over his cheek to his ear. "This isn't the kind of workout I had in mind when I came back here..."

His body hardened and pulsed. She was teasing him. That turned him on even more. He nodded. "That's right. You came here to lift, right?"

Her eyes narrowed with feigned irritation. "I do lift," she told him.

He dropped the towel on one end and lifted his hand to her shoulder. He gripped her bare skin, then skimmed his palm over her biceps. She flexed for him. And he grinned appreciatively. "You do lift."

"I have to be ready for anything," she said.

"To follow up on your lead?" he asked. She'd mentioned it during the meeting. But he hadn't been certain if she was telling the truth or trying to impress his team.

Or intimidate them.

She shook her head. "I was talking about last night."

She obviously preferred to talk about that than whatever she was working on. Maybe because it already hadn't panned out. "Were you trying to trace the source of the hay?" he asked her. "I've been trying that for months. There are too many farmers around here—too many unsecured barns—to find out where those bales are coming from..."

And more than half the population of Northern Lakes owned pickup trucks because of the rough winters, so anyone could throw a few stolen bales in the back and drive off with them.

She nodded. "Lab reports say the hay has come from different sources."

"Different farms, same arsonist," he remarked.

She nodded again. "I have to be ready for *him*."

Last night had proved she was ready for anything. She'd helped put out that fire. She glanced up at him and pulled her bottom lip between her teeth, as if she wondered if she was ready for Braden, too.

But he wasn't ready for her. Both his personal and professional lives were a mess. He had no business starting anything with anyone. Then again, it had already started with Sam—the moment they'd met.

"Show me," he challenged her. And he tugged her over to the bench he'd just been using.

She sat on it, then lay back and stared up at the barbell. "I can't lift that," she admitted.

He popped a couple of weights off both ends of the bar. "Is that light enough?"

She glared at him and wrapped her hands around the bar. She adjusted her grip and then lifted—far more easily than he'd thought she would be able. But he kept his hands beneath the bar, ready to catch it in case she needed help. After doing a few reps, sweat beaded on her brow. An errant bead rolled down her neck while more moisture gathered along her cleavage.

He could see the shadow between her breasts and the outlines of her nipples beneath the thin tank top and exercise bra. He wanted to touch her. He waited until she put the bar into the holders. Then he stroked her arms again, as if measuring her biceps. He moved his fingertips up to her shoulders, then over the slopes of her breasts.

She sucked in a breath. "Braden…"

He stilled, waiting to see if she'd said his name in protest. Or...

She arched off the bench, as if begging for his touch. So he touched. He moved his hands over her breasts. They were too big for him to cup in his palms. Her nipples tightened and pressed against the thin fabric of her clothes. But it was still too much. He wanted to see her with nothing covering her but his hands. Nothing but his body.

He reached for the bottom of her shirt and started inching up the tank top. Her eyes darkened, the pupils swallowing all the blue, as she watched him, as she waited for him to undress her.

But suddenly, she tensed. Maybe she'd changed her mind. Then he heard it, too. The creak of a door opening and the echo of footsteps against the concrete.

It could have been one of the Hotshots coming back to check on him or to convince him to join them at the bar. But the footsteps weren't quick with the purpose and assurance with which his team usually moved. These footsteps were measured, almost furtive, as if whoever had walked into the firehouse didn't want to be discovered.

Sam looked at him with the same concern he felt. Had the arsonist come back to leave another note—or set another fire?

8

Predictably, Braden tried to step in front of her as they exited the workout room. Sam didn't need his protection, though. He needed hers. So she elbowed him aside and led the way into the hall with her gun. She'd retrieved it from the bag she'd brought into the workout room with her. After the fire last night, she knew to keep her weapon with her at all times.

With a clang and a clatter, something fell over inside the firehouse. She tightened her grasp on the Glock. But she had to race to beat Braden down the hallway. She didn't think he was just being overprotective of her now. He was protecting his house. And he was pissed the arsonist might have had the guts to come back.

She swung her barrel toward where the noise had emanated, and the space flooded with light as Braden switched on the overhead fluorescents. The light bounced off the bald head of a man who fumbled for the weapon on his belt.

"You don't need the gun," Sam told Trooper Gingrich as she lowered her barrel. "I'm not going to shoot you." Although she was tempted…

Her body hummed with tension that had less to do with thinking the arsonist had returned to the firehouse. She was vibrating with the memory of how Braden had been touching her. And how she'd wanted him to keep touching her...

"I'm sorry I interrupted you two," Gingrich snidely remarked as his gaze flickered over her workout attire and Braden's bare chest.

"What the hell are you doing here?" Braden asked.

Sam suspected she knew. "He came to see me."

His face, which had gone white when she'd pointed the gun at him, turned ruddy now with anger. "Damn right I came to see you," he replied. "I went by your motel, then saw your rental car parked outside."

Tourism season had pretty much wrapped up in the quaint little northern town of a million lakes. So hers was probably one of the only vehicles with a rental sticker and plate parked along the streets.

Braden stepped forward, like he had earlier, every muscular inch of his sexy body tense with anger and defensiveness. "Don't talk to her like that!" he admonished the other man. "What are you—pissed off she didn't buy into your ridiculous accusations? What do you think I did last night? Throw that Molotov cocktail on a boomerang so it would fly back into my house?"

Sam choked back a laugh. Braden had done a good job shooting the trooper down. But the officer hadn't been completely off base. While Braden wasn't setting the fires, it was quite possible he knew the person who was.

Maybe even the person standing in front of him right now.

She resisted the urge to raise her gun again. She felt nearly as protective of Braden as he seemed to feel of her. But according to his team, Braden was protective of everyone. This feeling was new to her.

"This has nothing to do with you," she assured Braden. "The trooper is mad at me."

"Damn right!" Gingrich yelled. "I want to know why the hell you asked my sergeant for my dash-cam video from last night!"

Remembering how he'd spoken to her like she was stupid, Sam replied just as patronizingly, "Because I want to check your alibi for the fire last night."

Martin's breath whooshed out as though she'd shot him—right in the stomach. He nearly doubled over. "What? Why..."

Braden chuckled, but then reached out and almost comfortingly patted his old rival's shoulder. "Doesn't feel so good, huh? To be accused of something you didn't do?"

She turned toward Braden in surprise and asked, "You don't believe he did it?" Because she wasn't as convinced.

Gingrich sucked in a breath to replace the air he'd lost. He didn't need to answer Braden's question. It was clear from his ruddy complexion and tense body that he didn't appreciate the accusation.

"So did you bring the video?" she asked.

He shook his head. "No," he grumbled. "But my supervisor emailed it to you."

"Good." While she'd brought her bag with the gun into the workout room, she'd left her laptop in the women's locker room when she'd changed out of her street clothes.

"But you don't need to look at it," he told her. "I wasn't anywhere near Zimmer's place last night."

She shrugged. "Then the video will prove that." And she could rule him out as a suspect and focus on the Hotshots.

His bald head jerked now like he had a nervous tic.

"You can't watch it!" he exclaimed. "You have to take my word for it that I wasn't anywhere near him."

She laughed at that. "If I had a dollar for every time a suspect told me I had to take his word for something..." She would own a house instead of renting a small studio apartment. No, she probably wouldn't. The studio was just fine for the little amount of time she was actually home. Like her dad and brothers, she went where the fires were being set. And like them, she put them out, too. But in an entirely different way.

Why couldn't they respect that? Why couldn't they respect her? Maybe once she'd been doing it longer...

Maybe once she caught more arsonists...

This one was important—not just to keep Braden and Northern Lakes safe, but also because her father had asked her to look into the fires. Mack had never done that before. He'd never asked *her* for anything.

"What's on that video has nothing to do with the fires," Gingrich insisted.

Sam narrowed her eyes and studied his ruddy face. "Then why don't you want me to see it?"

"I don't want *anyone* to see it," he said, his voice rising with panic.

Braden chuckled almost gleefully. "Oh, I've got to see this, too."

There was something on there, something incriminating, even if it didn't have anything to do with the fires. "I'm an officer, too," Sam said. "If you're doing something illegal, I'll have to turn you in."

He shook his head. "It's not illegal."

"Then I don't understand why you're so worried about it," she said. There had been instances of dash-cam video that made internet sensations of officers caught lip-synching and things like that. But she suspected Martin wasn't worried about such embarrassment.

"I'm a married man," he said, lifting his hand where a ring circled one chubby finger. "What's on that video could change that."

She'd figured that stripper ringtone hadn't belonged to his wife. "If what I see—" and she was going to look at it no matter how much he begged "—isn't related to the arson investigation, nobody else will see the footage."

He didn't look reassured. "I've got kids," he said. "They're young. I can't put them through…"

Just what the hell did he have to hide? She couldn't wait to see that footage.

His head jerked again—toward Braden. "He definitely can't see it!"

Braden looked offended. "I won't tell anybody what's on it, either."

The trooper looked even less reassured. He looked downright frightened. Just what the hell was on that video?

Sam intended to find out. And Gingrich must have realized there was no way he could change her mind, because he turned and slunk off toward the door.

Maybe she should've thanked him before he left—not for the video, since he hadn't brought that, but for interrupting what had been going on in the workout room.

She'd lost her focus again. She'd let Braden's sweaty bare chest distract her as much as his freshly showered bare chest had. And when he'd touched her, she'd lost her mind entirely. She needed all her wits about her to catch this arsonist. She would not get stupid over Braden Zimmer again.

BRADEN SHOULD HAVE been relieved that Sam hadn't wanted to return to the workout room. He couldn't afford to be distracted right now—not when he'd become the target of the arsonist. He had to stay sharp and focused. But his focus kept returning to Sam—to how she would have looked without her workout clothes, of how she would have tasted had he kissed her skin…

No. He wasn't relieved. He was damn well disappointed, which was stupid. He had no business messing around with Mack's daughter with an arsonist on the loose. He would only put her in more danger.

His only focus had to be catching the arsonist—before it was too late.

Was Marty telling the truth? Did whatever was on the video have nothing to do with the fires?

Braden intended to find out. He showered quickly. But Sam probably didn't have to; she'd only lifted the barbell a few times. So he wasn't surprised when there was no response to his knock on the door to the women's locker room.

Had she gone back to her motel? He hurried down the stairs and headed toward his office where he'd left his keys. A light glowed inside, and he pushed open the door, which hadn't been locked.

Damn it. He was as bad as Stanley with forgetting to lock the doors. Sam glanced up from the computer she had on his desk while she sat in his old duct-taped leather recliner. She reached for the screen to pull it closed. But he caught it, holding it open.

He sucked in a breath at what he saw. Gingrich was making out with a woman on the hood of his patrol car. That woman wasn't his wife. But she had once been Braden's.

"You know her," Sam said. It wasn't a question. Either she'd guessed or she'd looked up his ex as a potential suspect.

He nodded. "Yeah, that's my ex-wife."

"That's why Gingrich didn't want you to see it," she said.

Braden wasn't sure. "Seems like he would have loved rubbing this in my face."

"It was enough for him that he knew," Sam surmised.

Braden's guts knotted with disgust. "That's why he always acted so smug around me, like there was something he knew that I didn't."

Sam nodded. "That patronizing smugness is why I suspected he could be the arsonist."

"No," Braden said. "If he hated me that much, he wouldn't have waited all these years before he started burning stuff down."

"I don't know…" she murmured as if she still had her suspicions.

He pointed toward the screen. "This proves he couldn't have started that fire last night."

She tilted her head and studied the time stamped on the video. "Oh, you'd be surprised how easily some irrefutable alibis can be refuted—how time stamps can be messed with…"

Braden's blood chilled. "But he didn't want us to see this."

"We can't be sure," she said. "Most criminals are really great liars. This might be exactly what he wanted us—you especially—to see." She gestured at the screen where the two people were awkwardly sliding around on the hood. "Why get involved with her? That had to be to get back at you."

Braden wasn't sure which one of them was getting back at him, though. It was almost as if Ami turned toward the camera and posed, making sure that whoever watched the video would see her.

How had he been such a fool? He'd married her. He'd intended to start a family with her. But he hadn't really known her at all.

Sam snapped the screen closed and slid her laptop into the bag sitting next to his chair. "I'll send this video off to an FBI lab and make sure it hasn't been tampered with," she assured him. Then she rose from his chair so she stood next to him.

He uttered a ragged sigh. "I can't call *him* the idiot anymore," Braden said.

"He's risking his marriage—his family—for a fling," Sam said. "He is the idiot."

"She's married, too," Braden said. "Her new husband hired a private detective who was staying at Serena Beaumont's boardinghouse. He thought she was coming to Northern Lakes to cheat on him with *me*."

Sam laughed. "That's karma…"

Braden shrugged shoulders that still felt weighed down by his own foolishness. He couldn't help but wonder how long Ami had been seeing Marty. He'd thought there had only been the guy she'd left him for. Now he wondered—how many others had there been?

"How didn't I notice what was going on right under my nose?" he asked.

Sam stared up at him, her beautiful blue eyes soft with sympathy. "You were busy," she said. "Leading your team, fighting fires all over the country, even as far as Canada. You weren't home much."

He wondered now if she was defending him or another man. He'd heard some of Mack's story. The guy was legendary not just as a smoke jumper base leader but for doing all that while raising his kids alone.

"And you trusted her," Sam added.

"I shouldn't have," Braden said. After Ami, he wouldn't find it easy to trust anyone else again. Not Sam…

"I wonder who else I shouldn't have trusted," he said. "You better check out my team. Maybe I've missed something—like I missed that."

"I already am checking out your team," she admitted. "It's too much of a coincidence that the fires only happen when you're in town."

He knew it was true. But like Ami's affairs, he hadn't wanted to face it. "I'd just assumed my team was the target—that the arsonist was after one or possibly all of them."

"Maybe he is," she agreed. "But one of them could be going after another. Maybe they resent Wyatt and Dawson being promoted to assistant or how Cody quickly became such a valuable team member…"

His guts tightened with dread—because he couldn't deny it was possible. He was also impressed with how well she knew his team already. "Well, you know it's not one of those three…"

"Or you," she added.

"Who do you suspect?"

She didn't reply, but it was obvious from her guarded expression that she had someone in mind.

"Who do you suspect?" he asked again.

She shook her head.

"Why won't you tell me?" he asked. "Do you think I'll tip them off to your investigation?"

"I think you're very protective of your team," she said.

"So yes." The knot of his guts tightened more. The woman frustrated him—sexually and professionally. "I wouldn't cover for them if one was committing a crime." Did she really think he would?

"But would you be able to face it?"

Damn. The woman was as good a judge of character as her father was. "You think that because of my ex—because I couldn't face her cheating?"

Sam shrugged. "You must have loved her a lot," she mused.

How could he have loved her? He hadn't even really known her.

"Do you miss her?" Sam asked.

He shook his head. He didn't miss Ami. But he missed that feeling—missed thinking he was in love. Now he realized it was just infatuation, attraction. He felt that again now, but a hundred times more intensely with Sam.

"Of course not," he said.

"My dad missed my mom," she said. "I think he still does. He must, or he would have gotten involved with someone else after she left."

"He was busy," Braden reminded her. "With his family, with his job. And maybe he figured if she wouldn't stay because of his life, that no one else would, either."

She stared at him intently now. "Is that what you think?" she asked. "That no one else will stay with you?"

He shrugged. "I don't know what to think anymore."

"Your guys want you to start dating again," she said. "They want you to be happy."

"They want me to have sex," Braden said with a mirthless chuckle. "They think I'll mellow out then."

Sam tilted her head as if considering it.

He shook his head. "We can't," he told her.

"Why not?" she asked.

His heart jumped in his chest. Did she want him as much as he wanted her? Except for the drunken women who'd tried to tear off his clothes, he hadn't felt very desirable until now.

Ami had bruised his ego more than his heart.

But he was more worried about his heart than his ego with Sam McRooney. "Are you staying in Northern Lakes?" he challenged her.

She smiled. "You're so old-fashioned."

He flinched.

"Most men would love that I'm not staying," she said. "That they don't have to pretend to want a future with me."

He worried that he wouldn't have to pretend, either. That he might… "So you're not staying?"

She shook her head. "Of course not. The only thing for me here is the arsonist. Once I catch him, I'll leave."

Braden felt a jab in his heart and held his breath. At least she was honest with him. There was nothing for her here.

"I mean career-wise," she clarified. "There's nothing for me in Northern Lakes once I wrap up this case. I'm based out of DC. My apartment is there. My life."

"My life is here," he said. "My job. My team. My home. I grew up here and want to raise a family here."

"You want to get married again?" she asked, as if the idea surprised her.

He hadn't given it much thought after Ami had left, but now he nodded. "Yes, I do." His parents had a great marriage. He knew it was possible—if you found the right person. "I guess I am old-fashioned. I want to have kids, too."

She shuddered as if the mere thought of children scared her. "We really have nothing in common," she said.

"So we can't get involved," he said. He wanted someone who would stay in Northern Lakes—someone who would be the partner his mother was to his father. He wanted to be a team raising kids, nurturing and loving them together.

And he wanted those kids before he got much older. He wanted to be able to keep up with them when they were teenagers, wanted to be young enough to play with his grandkids like his dad and mom played with theirs.

"No, we can't get serious," she agreed even as she lifted her arms and linked her fingers behind his neck. She rose up on tiptoe and touched her lips to his throat— it was the farthest she could reach. Her breath whispered warmly across his skin as she suggested, "But we can have a fling."

He laughed, thinking she was kidding. But she pulled his head down until her lips met his. She kissed him hungrily, her mouth greedy. She nipped at his lips and slid her tongue into his mouth.

Breathing heavily, he stepped back and shook his head. "We can't do this." For so many reasons.

"You need this," she said. "You need to just have some fun—relieve some tension."

It sounded good. Hell, it sounded exciting and sexy. And dangerous, too. He shook his head. "It's too dangerous. If anyone thinks there's something going on between us…"

"You mean the arsonist?"

"Yes. He would go after you, too," Braden said, "like he went after Avery and Serena. Being with me would put you in danger."

She nodded in agreement.

"Not to mention that Mack will kill me," he added.

She tensed. "Did my father tell you to stay away from me?" she asked.

"No," Braden said. "He told me to keep you safe." And

Braden knew that the only way he would be able to do that was to stay away from her.

As much as he wanted her, he couldn't have her.

9

SAM WASN'T ABOUT to let Braden walk away from her out of some self-sacrificing sense of obligation. She fisted her hand in his black T-shirt and tugged him toward her.

"We just agreed this is a bad idea," he said. But he didn't pull away.

"It's only a bad idea if someone finds out," she said. "Gingrich and Ami have kept their…" She didn't know what to call what she'd witnessed on that dash-cam footage. "They kept it secret and they're idiots."

Something leaped in Braden's eyes, like a flame in the dark. Desire. But his mouth curved into a faint grin. "I'm an idiot, too."

"We've all been stupid for love before," she said.

"You, too?"

She sighed. "Oh, I've made my share of mistakes."

"Am I going to be another one of those?"

She was afraid he might be, but she wanted him too much to let fear dissuade her. "You do make me stupid," she admitted.

"We need all our wits about us now," Braden said. "We need to make sure the arsonist doesn't come after you."

She laughed. "Oh, he will. But it will have nothing

to do with you. I'm investigating him. I'm coming after him. He's going to try to take me out over everyone else. That's why Mack asked you to keep me safe. He knows I'm in danger just being here."

Braden reached out then, skimming his fingertips along her bruised cheek. "I don't want you getting hurt," he said. "But I want you..." He stepped closer until his body touched hers almost everywhere. "I want you..."

"Then take me," she told him. In the workout room she'd waited for him to touch her, to undress her. She was too impatient to wait now. She wanted him too much. So she pulled off her own clothes until she stood before him naked.

His breath whistled out between his teeth. "You are so damn beautiful..."

The way he looked at her, so hungrily, made her feel beautiful, sexy...

"Now you," she told him as she reached for the bottom of his shirt.

"You've already seen me naked but for a towel," he reminded her.

"I want to see all of you," she said. After pulling off his shirt, she reached for his belt.

But he caught her hands and stopped her to take over. He undressed quickly. And now she knew what the towel had been hiding. He was long and heavy and hard.

Her breath escaped in a lustful sigh of appreciation. "Your ex-wife was crazy," she said. Why would any woman cheat on him? Why settle for a pudgy bald guy like Marty when she'd had male perfection like Braden? "You are incredible."

He leaned down and kissed her, as if her compliments had embarrassed him. Or excited him...

He excited her, too, teasing her with his tongue. He

swept it across her bottom lip. But he didn't slide it into her mouth—just tempted her with the tip of it—while the head of his cock just touched the underside of her breast.

He was so tall. And she was not. But then he lifted her onto the edge of his desk. Her feet swung above the floor. She lifted her legs and tried to lock them around his waist and pull him toward her—into her.

But he was intent on taking his time with her. While he kissed her, he moved his hands over her body. He stroked her breasts, rubbing his thumbs across the sensitive tips.

Passion overwhelmed her, emanating from her nipples to spread hotly throughout her body. Her clit pulsed and throbbed. She needed release. She needed Braden. She clutched at his shoulders, trying to pull him toward her.

But he stepped back, then dropped to his knees. He parted her legs and pressed a kiss to the sensitive skin on the inside of her thigh. Her whole leg tingled, and that pulsing in her core increased to a frenzy. She needed him so badly that a whimper slipped between her lips.

But he took his time, kissing her other thigh, trailing his lips sensually up and down the length of it.

"Braden…"

He glanced up at her. His face was flushed, his dark eyes bright. He looked like he wanted her as desperately as she wanted him. But he held on to his control, moving his mouth up her thigh to the sexual heart of her. He flicked his tongue across her clit—back and forth.

Her body trembled. "Braden…"

His hands were back on her breasts, stroking the curves while his thumbs rubbed the ultrasensitive nipples. Then his tongue stroked her, sliding inside her.

She shuddered as an orgasm rippled through her body. "Braden!"

His control finally snapped. Jerking open a desk

drawer, he grabbed a condom from the box and murmured, "Remind me to thank Cody," and sheathed his cock. Then he nudged the tip of it against her.

Thanks to him, she was wet and ready. But as he entered her, she had to arch and stretch to take him deeper—he was so big. And he felt so good. She held his shoulders, then stroked her fingers down the bulging muscles in his arms.

He'd lifted that heavy barbell so easily—just as easily as he'd lifted her onto the desk. The metal surface might have been hard and cold beneath her, but she didn't notice. She didn't notice anything but the sensation of him moving inside her.

She lifted her legs and locked them around his waist as he quickened the pace. His jaw was clenched, but then he leaned down and kissed her. His mouth was hungry on hers, nipping at her lips.

It was all too much for Sam. Tension wound inside her, spiraling before it broke. Her body shuddered as she came again and kept coming. She uttered a soft scream as pleasure overwhelmed her.

Then Braden groaned, and his big body tensed. Finally he came, pumping his hips frantically as an orgasm claimed him. He leaned his forehead against hers, both of them damp with sweat.

He stared down at her, but she couldn't read the expression in his dark eyes.

A FEW DAYS LATER, she still had no idea what he had been thinking. She couldn't get that night out of her head no matter where she was, but most especially not here—in the office where it had happened.

If not for needing to use his computer, she might not have come back into the small space with its cement-block walls. It was almost as if she could smell it here. The perspiration from their writhing bodies, the sex…

She shuddered again as her body began to pulse. She'd thought having sex with him would remove the distraction. She wouldn't be wondering and wanting once she knew what it was like to be with him. But now that she knew, she only wanted him more.

So she'd been sticking to the motel, focusing on the investigation. Trent Miles had an alibi. When that first fire had started in Northern Lakes, it hadn't been wildfire season yet, so Trent had been at his off-season job—as a firefighter in Detroit. She'd found news footage of him working a fire there.

Ethan Sommerly had no such alibi. As usual, he'd been alone, with no one but possibly some bears to vouch for his whereabouts. She'd also checked Owen James's EMT call logs. There hadn't been one the other night—he hadn't rushed out on a call when he'd left the bar.

What had he been doing? Following his boss? Waiting for the precise moment to throw his IED?

It could be either one of the men. But why? Had one applied for an assistant position and been denied? Or was one of them after Braden's job? She had to find the motive, so she was going through Braden's personnel records now, reading everyone's files. But then she stumbled across another file. "Hmm…" she murmured.

A soft groan followed. Startled, she glanced up and found Braden leaning against the doorjamb of his office, studying her. "Are you watching porn?" he asked.

She laughed. "Why would you think that? Do you have some on this computer?"

He shook his head. "It was just that sound you made…"

It must have reminded him of that night—just like she'd been reminded the moment she stepped into the office. His gaze moved from her to the desk. He was definitely on the same page, thinking about what they'd done.

He lifted his hand and squeezed the back of his neck. His handsome face twisted into a grimace of pain.

"What's wrong?" she asked as she stood and approached him. Had he been hurt?

He shook his head. "Just feeling a little edgy…"

"I thought we took care of that the other night," she murmured.

"This is a different kind of edgy," he said. "It's this feeling I get sometimes…"

"Your sixth sense about fires?"

He shrugged. "I don't know what it is exactly. How'd you know about it? Gingrich?"

"He thinks it's hocus-pocus," she said. Fortunately since they'd watched his dash-cam video, he'd been scarce. Maybe it was legit, but she had yet to get confirmation of that from the FBI lab. Other officers had been patrolling Northern Lakes in case the arsonist struck again. She still would prefer Braden to have around-the-clock protection, but he had refused.

Maybe he would change his mind if she offered again. She wouldn't mind being with him around the clock—especially at night. The past couple of nights she'd just tossed and turned, tangling her blankets around her. She could have blamed the lumpy motel mattress, but she knew who was really to blame.

Braden. She leaned toward him, needing the warmth of his body—just needing his body.

"What do you think?" he asked.

She blinked up at him, confused. "About?"

"My sixth sense? Hocus-pocus?" he asked, his voice light as if it didn't matter. But his face was tense, and his eyes dark as he stared down at her.

"I believe you," she said. "My dad has the same thing, but about people, not fires."

Braden and her dad were too much alike. She'd never had the daddy issues some women had, where they sought out men exactly like their fathers. She was more likely to seek out someone exactly the opposite of her father. But that hadn't worked out well for her, either.

"That's good," he said. "That you don't think I'm crazy, or worse yet, criminal."

The only thing that was criminal about Braden Zimmer was how damn sexy he was. It wasn't fair. It wasn't fair how hot he was and how hot he made her. She wanted him again. So badly…

"I think I'm the crazy one," she murmured. He'd made her feel that way—made her needy in a way she'd never been before. She reached out. As her fingertips touched his chest, a siren rang out—like she'd touched a masterpiece at the museum and set off an alarm. Of course, she'd seen him without his shirt; his chest was something of a masterpiece of sculpted muscle.

Braden cursed. "There's a fire."

His sixth sense about fires was even more accurate than her father's sixth sense about people. Her father had certainly never had any sense of who she was or what she was capable of. "You were right."

He sighed. "I'd rather be wrong than have the arsonist strike again."

"You don't know that it's the arsonist," she reminded him. But she intended to find out.

"You're not coming," Braden argued. But Sam was already stepping into the pants and boots Hank had tossed at her. The female Hotshot's extra pair were still too big for the petite blonde, though. The jacket hung loosely on her, too.

"I need to be there," Sam replied.

"We don't know if the arsonist set this fire," he said. "But if he did, I can send someone back for you."

She shook her head. "That'll take too long. Too much evidence could be lost."

He flinched, knowing she was referring to his not calling her immediately when he'd found that hay bale. If he'd called her sooner, the arsonist might not have had the chance to torch it. Braden had nearly lost his house that night.

Of course, the structure could be repaired. If he'd lost Sam…

His heart slammed against his ribs, pounding harder at the horrific thought.

That was why he couldn't allow her to ride along now. But she was already climbing into the truck. Cody, damn him, had held out a hand to help her up the big first step onto the engine.

The truck started to pull through the open door, so he jumped aboard, too. As he settled onto one of the jump seats, he glared at Sam and the others. Cody shrugged, as if he'd been helpless to resist her.

That was the way Braden had felt the other night. Even though he'd known he was breaking his promise to Mack and potentially putting her in danger, he hadn't been able to resist her. He just hoped he wasn't putting her in danger again.

One way he could prevent that was by staying informed. "Fill me in," Braden told Wyatt. Dawson drove the rig.

"Call came in—brush fire out near the campgrounds."

Fear clenched Braden's stomach. The first arson hadn't

started there, but it had spread that far. And the arsonist had restarted fires out that way.

"It's him, isn't it?" Cody asked. But the question was directed at Sam—not Braden.

"If it is," Sam said, "he's escalating. The fire at Braden's was just a few nights ago."

If he was escalating, that meant he was suddenly all the more deadly.

"Did you call up the machines?" Braden asked. He'd been preoccupied with Sam when the call had come in; he had no idea what his men had done. But he could trust that they wouldn't have left had they not been ready.

Wyatt nodded. "Of course."

"I can run a dozer," Sam offered. But she waited, like she thought Braden would reject her help.

He'd rather have her driving the dozer than trying to man the hose, though. He wanted her far from the flames. But as they neared the site, he realized that would be difficult. The fire was spreading. Thankfully another engine followed theirs.

The team was all still in Northern Lakes. He'd known that big fire was coming. He'd felt it even before Sam had arrived in town, even before he'd found that note on his desk. He'd known the fire the other night wasn't it. But he had a strange feeling this wasn't it, either.

Because that edginess was still niggling at him...

Smoke filled the sky, turning it black despite the sun shining high overhead. Flames shimmered and danced as they ate at the trees. Some of those trees were already charred from previous fires; others snapped and crackled as the fire consumed their brightly colored leaves.

Several Hotshots manned a hose, training the burst of water onto the flames. Others drove machinery, knocking down the burning trees with the dozer while a back-hoe tore up the ground, cutting a break to stop the fire.

With the whole crew working it, they fought back the flames quickly until only smoke rose from the black-ened earth. After the fire was out, Sam walked the site, inspecting every ember like a fortune-teller reading tea leaves in the bottom of a porcelain cup.

How did she manage to look sexy even in the oversize gear? She managed to be hot with soot smeared across her face. Finally she walked back toward the truck.

"So?" he asked before Cody could again.

She shook her head.

"What?"

"Looks like a campfire wasn't put out," she said. "I don't think it's the arsonist."

Braden had already deduced the same. That explained why his edginess hadn't eased. But maybe that edginess had nothing to do with the arsonist and everything to do with Sam and how much he wanted her.

They were all quiet on the ride back—almost as if they were disappointed the arsonist hadn't been behind the fire. If he had, Sam might've found a clue to his identity. Now they were no closer to catching him than they'd already been.

But then he remembered how Sam had looked staring at his computer. And that sound she'd made...

She'd found something in his records. Fear clutched his stomach that it could be one of his team setting those fires.

Then he heard a shout from the front seat of the rig. Dawson was his strong, silent assistant. He rarely spoke, let alone yelled.

"What is it?" Braden asked.

Dawson just pointed toward the windshield. Braden stared ahead and saw it, too. Smoke. Pluming up from the firehouse.

10

THE SMOKE HAD risen all the way to the third-floor conference room. Despite the breeze blowing through the open windows, and the fact that nearly twenty-four hours had passed, the odor still permeated the space. The smell of it tickled Sam's nose and the back of her throat.

Fortunately the flames had not made it above the bales of hay they'd found burning in one of the bays when they'd returned from the campfire call. The ceiling in the garage was too high for the fire to have spread.

They'd put it out with just the hose Stanley used to wash the trucks. Thankfully Stanley and Annie hadn't been in the garage. He'd taken the dog for a walk. But of course he'd left the door open when he'd left, as he so often did. Braden glanced up from his lectern and noticed her standing in the doorway. He gestured for her to take his spot.

She had something to say, but probably not what they wanted to hear. All the Hotshots stared at her as she walked the length of the room. But no one threw questions at her today. They were subdued.

They had been attacked at their heart—at their home base.

Even though no one had asked the question aloud, Sam answered it. "No leads," she said. "My earlier lead didn't pan out, either."

"Gingrich had an alibi?" Owen James asked. He'd attended the same school as Braden and Martin, so he understood their rivalry better than anyone. Had he shared in it? Like Gingrich, did he resent Braden—envy him already making Hotshot superintendent?

Braden was handsome, smart, commanding. And loyal. Too bad that loyalty wasn't returned to him. First his ex-wife had cheated on him. Now a member of his team might be threatening his livelihood and his life.

Anger coursed through Sam, heating her blood. But she had no business being angry with a woman she'd never met. So she would focus all that anger on the arsonist. "We will catch him."

"Heard that before..." someone murmured. It may have been Ethan Sommerly; his beard was so bushy it was hard to tell if his lips had moved. What was he trying to hide with all that hair?

She had been able to find out very little about him from his personnel files. While Owen James had applied to be an assistant superintendent, Ethan had never tried for a promotion. But that didn't mean he didn't have a motive for arson. Sometimes the motive was only madness.

"Sam has only been on this assignment for less than a week," Braden said, jumping to her defense as usual. Maybe it was such a part of his character that he just couldn't help himself.

But still, remembering all the times her dad and brothers had tried to protect her, Sam bristled. "I asked your superintendent to call this meeting today, not to discuss the investigation specifically, but to talk about your protection," she said. "I think yesterday proved none of you are safe."

"We haven't been safe for a while," Cody said.

Dawson and Wyatt nodded in agreement.

"That's why I asked the state police to provide more than extra patrols."

Hank snorted. "Like those did any good yesterday."

The officer on duty hadn't seen a thing. They'd found the fire before he'd even noticed the smoke. Of course he'd been inside the coffee shop a few blocks away.

"I asked that they station an officer at the firehouse around the clock."

Braden shook his head. "No. That's not necessary."

She ignored his protest. "That's still not enough, though," she said. "I think all of you need extra protection."

Ethan Sommerly shook his head. "I'll just return to the UP. Nobody bothers me there."

She couldn't help thinking that he was hiding out in the woods. From what? Her?

Trent Miles snorted. "Yeah, I'm safer in Detroit."

"We don't need extra protection," Owen James said. "Not when we have each other. If we all stick together, we'll keep one another safe."

Not if one of them was the threat. That file she'd found on Braden's computer, regarding all the workplace accidents, had given her reason to suspect it was one of them. The fire yesterday hadn't changed her mind.

They hadn't all ridden together on that one engine. There had been another one as well as the truck and trailer with the heavy equipment. Who'd driven that? A few other guys had come in their individual pickups, Ethan Sommerly and Owen James included.

Either of them could have stayed behind and lit the hay bales after everyone else had left. She couldn't remember exactly when they'd shown up at the fire; it had been much later. Or maybe one of them came back early to set the firehouse fire. She'd been so focused on determining the origin of what turned out to be a campfire that she wouldn't have noticed if had someone slipped away.

Ethan sighed but nodded in agreement. "I'll stay. But you need to catch this guy."

"Killing you to be social?" Trent teased him.

He shuddered and nodded again.

A few of the Hotshots chuckled. But they were all still uneasy.

Sam was, too. "You need more protection," she said, maybe even from each other. "The arsonist is growing more and more dangerous."

"Nobody will protect us like we will each other," Owen insisted.

She doubted that—not when the arsonist could be among them.

"We'll be fine."

Every one of them assured Sam of the same thing as they exited the conference room. Braden hadn't dismissed them. But then he hadn't called the meeting; she had. And she didn't have their respect yet. She needed to earn it, and the only way she would do that was by catching the arsonist.

Unless he was one of them, then they would probably all hate her—as if she were somehow responsible even though all she'd done was catch him.

After they were all gone, she uttered a ragged sigh.

"They're stubborn," Braden said. He closed and locked the door to the conference room so they were completely alone.

Her pulse quickened, though not only with desire. It was with anger, too. She glared at him. "I wonder where they get that..."

"They're right, though," he continued. "Nobody will protect them like they will one another."

She wasn't so sure. And her skepticism must have shown because he groaned. "After the fire yesterday, you can't still think it's one of them."

"We weren't all together the entire time," she said. The only Hotshots she could account for without a doubt were the ones already cleared because they could alibi one another. Cody. Wyatt. Dawson. And of course, Braden.

Hank had been with them in the engine as well. But that left fifteen others without solid alibis.

He shook his head. "It's not someone on my team."

"You asked me to investigate them," she reminded him. "You've had your doubts, too."

"Not after today," he said. "It wasn't possible for one of them to have set those hay bales on fire back here and help us fight the campfire."

"You refuse to believe you could have been wrong about someone on your team."

"Not at all," he said. "I considered it. And that was wrong. I shouldn't have doubted any of them—not for even a moment."

"You're safe with Wyatt and Dawson and Cody," she said. "You need to let one of them protect you. But we both know you won't. You're more worried about them than you are about yourself."

He didn't argue with her. He just shrugged, his broad shoulders rippling beneath his tight black T-shirt. "I'll be fine."

That anger she'd felt over what his ex-wife had done was redirected again—toward him. She smacked one of those muscular arms of his. "You are an idiot!"

His mouth dropped open as he stared down at her. "What's wrong?"

Everything. He wasn't going to protect himself, so he was going to get hurt. Or worse...

Her eyes stung, so she blinked hard. It had to be the smoke that still lingered in the room. It couldn't be because she was worried about him, about losing him.

It wasn't as if she actually had him. She barely knew him. But she didn't want anything to happen to him—or anyone else. But most especially not to Braden.

"You're an idiot," she repeated. "Because this was meant for you."

"Your meeting?"

That, too.

"The fire," she said. "First he tried to burn down the house you're living in, then he tried to burn down the house where you really live—your firehouse."

She expected Braden to be as angry as she was and for all his anger to be directed at the arsonist. But instead of bristling with rage, he grinned.

"Yeah..."

"You are an idiot," she murmured. "Or you're crazy."

BRADEN WAS CRAZY. About her...

But that was crazy, too. She wasn't planning on staying in Northern Lakes. So he couldn't get attached. But he couldn't stop staring at her, either. She wore a skirt today with tall suede boots and a black sweater. She was so damn beautiful.

Just looking at her took his breath away. He nodded in full agreement with her assessment. "I am crazy," he agreed.

"You act like you're happy about the arsonist starting a fire in the firehouse," she said, as if she was accusing him of something.

"I am," he said.

And she smacked him again. Instead of stinging, his skin tingled from the contact with hers. His body tensed as desire coursed through him. He wanted her. Badly.

But he forced himself to focus. "I'm happy because this proves none of my team members could've started that fire yesterday."

No matter how much he argued with her she seemed determined to think the worst of his team.

"You were out there, too," he reminded her. And he was damn glad that she had insisted on riding along. If she'd been back at the firehouse alone...

He shuddered to think about what might have happened to her, what the arsonist might have done to her. Was that why he'd come around when the rest of them had been gone? Had he been trying to catch her alone?

"We weren't all together every minute," Sam said. "Someone could have slipped away."

"Without anyone else noticing they were missing?" he scoffed. "It would have taken some time to drive back from the campfire, to drag the hay bales in from wherever they were stashed. And then start the fire—all without Stanley seeing a thing."

Sam's brow furrowed and she murmured, "Something isn't adding up..."

"I know," Braden said. "It wouldn't have been possible for one of my team members to have started that fire."

Sam nodded, but slowly. "I did look into other suspects," she said. "I think the timing of the rejection letters going out, turning down US Forest Service firefighter candidates, and the first fire wasn't a coincidence."

Braden sighed. He'd considered the same thing. "That was my first thought, too," he said. "There was one position and a multitude of candidates. Nearly a hundred letters went out."

"Did you investigate any of them?"

He nodded. "There was a guy who'd applied every year for the past ten years."

"Thomas Maynard?" she asked. She'd noticed that, too. "Why do you keep turning him down?"

"He isn't physically fit enough for the job," Braden said.

She flinched as if he'd struck a nerve, which was weird because he could attest that she was physically fit. Very fit and sexy…

But maybe not big or strong enough to be a Hotshot or a smoke jumper. Was that what she'd really wanted to be?

"I understand his frustration," she said. And he suspected that she had.

"Maynard isn't strong enough to do the job," Braden said. "I doubt he's even strong enough to lift those hay bales." Except maybe the small one Braden had tripped over in his living room.

"Was there anyone else who stood out to you from the rejected candidates?" Sam asked.

Braden sighed. He hated even mentioning the kid's name. It was clear that Matthew Hamilton had had nothing to do with the fires. But he'd thought of him for that first fire. "There was a young man Wyatt's been mentoring since he was a kid. Now Wyatt's engaged to his sister. So there's no way Matt would try to hurt him. Or any of us."

"Why was he mentoring him?"

Braden sighed again. "He got in trouble when he was a kid. That's why I had to turn him down for the job."

"He has a felony on his record?" she asked. And she tensed now. "For what? Starting fires?"

"No," he said. "Vandalism. He smashed the windows

out of the car and the house of one of his mom's boy-friends."

"That's vicious."

"So was the boyfriend," Braden said. "He'd beat up Matthew's mom. Matt was too young to protect her. It was his way of expressing his anger and frustration." He felt bad for the kid, that protecting his mother had had such a major impact on his future. But he'd found a new path—working at the nursing home. He'd arguably found his calling. He'd make a great registered nurse.

"The arsonist is expressing his anger and frustration, too," she said, "with the fires."

He shook his head. "It can't be Matthew," he said. Sure, he'd been upset, but he'd also understood why he'd been turned down. That wasn't the only reason it couldn't be him, though. "He has an alibi."

"I read that in your notes," she said. "Video footage from the hotel where his mom works."

"I know you don't put much credence in videos," he said. She'd sent off Gingrich's dash-cam feed to the FBI lab. "But his mom and the head of hotel security vouched for him as well."

"And Thomas Maynard's wife vouched for him," she said, "according to your notes."

They both knew an alibi witness could lie, especially since Mrs. Maynard was just one person who probably wanted to protect her husband. Was that what Sam had found on his computer yesterday?

He hadn't had a chance to ask about her discovery because of the fire alarm going off. "What else did you find yesterday?" he asked.

"The file with all the workplace accident reports," she said.

Braden shrugged. "Yeah..." Theirs was a dangerous

job; there were bound to be accidents. "We've had our share."

When they'd been clear-cutting areas to protect the forest from future fires, they'd stumbled across some spikes in trees that had caught the chainsaw blades. He was lucky no one had been hurt more than needing a few stitches. And the brakes on Cody's personal truck hadn't been the only ones to fail. Some of the other trucks had had mechanical issues.

"There were quite a few," she pointed out. "With injuries."

"Nothing serious." And he hadn't considered the accidents particularly serious, either. "You know that it's a hazardous job. Stuff happens."

She nodded, but that doubtful look was still on her face, furrowing her brow.

"You still think someone on my team might be the arsonist?" Braden asked. "Even though it would've been hard for someone to have slipped away yesterday?"

"Hard," she agreed, albeit reluctantly. "Not impossible. Nothing's impossible…"

"Do you think the arsonist might not be working alone?" he asked. That hadn't occurred to him until now.

"They usually act alone," she admitted. "The only pairs I've busted are the ones who start fires for profit. And there is no way anyone's profited from the fires here in Northern Lakes."

"Agreed," he said. His head pounded faintly with frustration over trying to figure out who the arsonist was. But his head wasn't the only thing pounding. His heart was, too, in reaction to her nearness and her beauty.

"I still think someone on your team could be dangerous," she insisted.

Braden shook his head. He'd doubted his team once,

and guilt still plagued him over that. He wouldn't doubt them again. "The only dangerous one on my team is me," he said as he stepped closer to her.

She arched a blond brow. "Who have you hurt?" she asked.

"Nobody yet," he admitted. "But I will hurt the arsonist when I get my hands on him. And I may hurt you."

She laughed and challenged him, "Try. I'm much tougher than I look."

"I won't be the one physically hurting you," he said. "The arsonist will—if he thinks we're seeing each other."

"We're not."

He stepped even closer. "We're not?"

He hadn't been able to get that night out of his mind—how she'd tasted, how she'd felt. He wanted her to admit it, too—that it had meant something to her. That he could mean something to her...

11

ONE MINUTE SHE was standing, the next Braden had lifted her onto the long conference table. Sam reached up, but not to push him away. She pulled him down with her.

She wanted him every bit as badly as he wanted her. She fumbled with his belt, dragging it free of his pants. Then she reached for his zipper.

He was pushing up her skirt and tugging down her panties. His fingers stroked over her core before easing inside her. She arched toward his hand, wanting more.

A moan rumbled in her throat. She grasped his shirt and dragged it off, over his head. Because she didn't want him to stop touching her, she pulled off her own sweater and unclasped her bra. She wanted to feel his chest against her—wanted to feel the soft hair over his muscles brushing over her nipples. She moaned again.

He kissed her, with so much passion. His lips played with hers, tugging and sliding over them. Then his tongue stroked across hers.

She clutched at him, trailing her short nails down his back. He groaned against her mouth, and his cock pushed through the boxers she hadn't yet been able to shove off.

He eased away from her just enough to pull down his

pants and underwear. Before he could tear open the condom packet he'd taken from a pocket, she touched him.

He was so long, so thick…

She wrapped her fingers around him and stroked up and down the length of his cock. He caught her wrist and, through gritted teeth, warned her, "If you keep that up, this'll be over too soon."

She smiled and was tempted to take care of him, the way he took care of everyone else all the time. But he was Braden. And he wasn't allowing that. He pushed her back onto the table, and he touched her everywhere—with his hands and his mouth. He kissed her shoulders and elbows and stomach.

She trembled as sensations raced over her. Her heart pounded frantically, with passion but also fear. Maybe he was right. Maybe she was in danger from him—just not the way he thought. Maybe she was in danger of falling for him…

No one had ever made love to her like Braden did. As thoroughly as he did. He loved her with his mouth and his tongue until her body shuddered and she screamed his name. Then she clutched at his shoulders and pulled him down onto her because even that orgasm hadn't been enough to quench her desire for him. She had to feel him inside her—filling her like he did. She arched her hips, meeting his thrusts.

They moved in unison, instinctively knowing what the other wanted—what the other needed. She wasn't surprised he seemed to have a sixth sense about it, like he had about fires. But she was a little surprised that she did—that she'd picked up instinctively on where he needed to be touched and kissed.

She moved her lips along his throat and chest and shoulder. And she trailed her hands down his back to grasp his tight ass. The man was perfect—every muscle so clearly defined. His body was so hard, so tense.

Tension wound tightly inside her, too. Though he'd given her one orgasm, she was ready for another—needed the kind of long, soul-shattering one he'd given her last time. She whimpered with frustration as the pressure built.

He reached between them and gently pushed his thumb against her pulsing clit, rubbing back and forth until she came.

Her world exploded as the orgasm shuddered through her body. Her toes curled; her every muscle contracted. She moaned his name again. Then he joined her, tensing and uttering a deep groan as he came.

He groaned again, panting for breath. Then he eased off her, pulling free. "I—I need to clean up," he murmured, as he headed toward the bathroom off the conference room.

Embarrassed, Sam hurriedly pulled her bra and panties back on and found her sweater. She wore her boots still and only had to pull her skirt down from around her waist.

That had been fast and frantic and fantastic.

And frightening as hell.

She couldn't fall for a man like Braden. His life was in Northern Lakes. He wouldn't shirk his responsibilities to his team; he would never leave to move to DC or anywhere else for that matter. This was where he'd grown up and where he'd raise his family and...

Sam wasn't even sure she wanted a family. She only remembered her father struggling—trying to find sitters for when he was gone, trying to handle them all on his own.

She didn't want that—she wanted the life she'd already built for herself. She didn't want Braden's life.

But she wanted Braden. Even after they'd made love like rabbits, she wanted him again. Wanted him so badly...

Panic pressed on her chest, making it difficult to breathe. She moved toward the open windows. Her face flamed as she realized someone might have heard them, might have realized what they were doing—what kind of conference they'd been having in the conference room.

She gulped in fresh air and glanced down to the street to see if anyone had been around to overhear. And she saw lights flashing. A patrol car was pulled up behind her rental. "What the hell...?"

"What?" Braden asked as he stepped from the bathroom.

She hurried past him and headed toward the stairs, nearly stumbling in her haste to descend. She didn't need a sixth sense to know that something bad had happened.

"WHAT IS IT?" Braden asked as he joined Sam and the state police officer next to her rental car. Shards of broken glass had sprayed across the asphalt on the driver's side.

The trooper turned reluctantly away from the sight of Sam's round ass straining against her skirt as she leaned through the open window. The glass had been knocked completely from the frame.

"Hey, Captain Zimmer," the trooper greeted Braden as most people did in Northern Lakes. Here he was known more for being the captain of the local fire department than the superintendent of the Huron Hotshots. "I noticed someone had broken the window on this vehicle."

Braden could see that much for himself. "What is it?" he asked Sam now as she eased through the frame and straightened, a piece of paper clasped in her hand.

The tightening of his stomach muscles told him what it was. A threat.

She held out the paper toward him, so he and the trooper could read it, too. The big blocky letters warned:

YOU NEED TO LEAVE NORTHERN LAKES. NOW. OR BAD THINGS WILL HAPPEN.

He was right. Being with him was putting her in danger. He waited until after she and the trooper finished their report. But when she moved to open the driver's door of her rental, he caught her arm and told her, "We need to talk."

Color flushed her face. Maybe she was angry about the broken window. Or maybe she was angry with him. Had he done something wrong?

Had he been too rough when he'd taken her on the conference room table? He'd never before lost control like he did with Sam.

She glanced around the street, as if concerned someone might overhear them. He didn't want to be overheard, either. He hadn't even wanted to think what he was thinking, much less speak it aloud.

"Let's go to my office," he said.

Her face flushed again, and her eyes darkened. And he knew she was thinking what he was—about how they'd gone at it on his desk.

Despite just having a body-numbing orgasm, he wanted her again. But he had to focus.

She shook her head. "I already told you that I'm not looking for a relationship," she said. "Your life is in Northern Lakes with your team. Mine is wherever the next arsonist strikes."

"I know," he conceded even as his guts tightened with

the realization. "I'm not looking for a relationship, either. I just got out of a real bad marriage."

Her face flushed a deeper shade of red. "You didn't want to talk about…"

"Us?" There couldn't be an *us*. They were both in agreement about that. So why did he feel so damn disappointed instead of relieved? "No, I want to talk about the arsonist." The only way to keep her safe was to catch the son of a bitch as soon as possible.

He led her back into the firehouse. The setting sun spilled light across the concrete through the open overhead door.

"I hope you're not feeling responsible for this note," she said as he closed the door behind her.

He was.

"I told you that he wouldn't want me here, investigating him," she said. "It wouldn't matter if I was a man or a married woman with kids—he was going to leave me one of these notes. He doesn't want me to catch him."

But the hard glint in her blue eyes indicated she was more determined than ever to do just that. The arsonist's stupid note hadn't scared her away; it had only pissed her off.

Braden sighed but nodded. "Probably…"

"I'm going to catch him," she said.

He nodded. "I believe you. But I want you to catch him faster."

Her anger was directed at him now; she glared. "I'm going as fast as I can."

"You're wasting your time checking out my workplace incident reports," he said. "Those kinds of things happen all the time. That's been going on for a while before the fires started."

"You just don't want it to be someone on your team."

"No, I don't," he agreed. And maybe that was why he struggled so hard to give her the name she hadn't yet mentioned herself. He'd wanted her to think of it on her own—wanted her to consider him a suspect—so Braden wouldn't feel so badly about it.

She narrowed her eyes and tilted her head, studying his face. "You have someone in mind."

He uttered a ragged sigh.

"And you don't want to tell me," she surmised.

"I wanted you to come up with the name yourself," he admitted.

"Your ex-wife?"

He gasped. "Ami? Not only does she have the same alibi as good ol' Marty. But why would she set the fires?"

"To get your attention? For spite?" Sam shrugged. "Because she's nuts?"

"She's not angry with me," he said. "She invited me to her wedding."

"Yeah, she's nuts."

He chuckled. "She doesn't want attention for setting fires. She wants attention for being beautiful, sexy..."

Sam tensed, and her voice was a little sharp when she replied, "Of course."

Was she jealous? She'd just told him she had no interest in a relationship with him. Why would she care that he thought his ex-wife was beautiful and sexy? There was no denying the obvious.

"No wonder her new husband hired that private investigator," she murmured.

"Because he knew he was an idiot to trust her," Braden said.

"Would you be an idiot for her again?" she asked. "Would you ever trust her again?"

He shook his head. And he wanted to reach out to

Sam, wanted to pull her into his arms and kiss her with the passion burning inside him. But she'd told him she didn't want anything more.

His pride be damned, he admitted, "The only woman I would be an idiot for again is you."

He'd already done that because he was afraid he was falling for her. Even knowing how impossible a relationship between them would be, he was falling...

But how could he help it? She was so beautiful, so smart, so strong...

A smile curled up the corners of her sexy mouth. "You make me stupid, too," she assured him.

He felt a little better that he wasn't in this alone—that she felt like a fool, too, for letting their feelings go further than they'd intended, further than the fling she'd offered him. He reached for her now, but she stepped back and shook her head.

"We have to keep our wits about us now," she said.

And she was right. They couldn't afford to be distracted. The arsonist was coming after her now.

Braden had promised Mack that nothing would happen to her. He intended to keep that promise.

He drew in a deep breath and nodded his agreement.

"So if it's not your ex-wife," she said, "who do you have in mind?"

He hesitated.

"I haven't heard back from the FBI lab yet, but it would have been hard for Gingrich to tamper with dash-cam footage," Sam admitted. "So I don't think he's a viable suspect."

"If he isn't, then neither is Ami." Gingrich hadn't been alone in that dash-cam footage. But Sam had forgotten that—almost as if she'd wanted his ex to be guilty.

"Yeah, yeah," she said dismissively. "So who is it? What name are you so reluctant to give me?"

He ran his hand down the back of his neck, trying to ease the tension. The campfire hadn't been it; neither had the burning hay bales in the firehouse. That big fire was still coming—he could feel it.

So if he had the chance to stop it, he had to. "There's only one person who has as much access to the firehouse as the team does. He's almost an unofficial member of the team."

The color drained from Sam's face as she realized who he meant. He didn't feel any better that she'd come up with the suspect on her own—or relatively on her own. He didn't want to believe it was him any more than he wanted it to be a member of his team.

"I hope we're wrong," he said.

She nodded. "Me, too."

12

SAM DIDN'T WANT this suspect to be guilty. But she had a job to do, so she had to interrogate Stanley. The curly-haired kid fidgeted in the chair across from hers in the conference room.

"What's wrong?" she asked as he wriggled on the chair.

"I've only been up here to clean before," he said. "It feels weird to be sitting here—where they all sit." He sounded as if he was in awe of the team.

But that didn't mean he wasn't capable of hurting them. Stalkers were often in awe of the objects of their obsession.

"Do you want to be a firefighter someday?" she asked him.

He had just turned eighteen shortly before that first fire had started. The same foster home where Cody Mallehan had lived before he'd turned eighteen had forced him out, too, so Cody brought the kid north, from Detroit to Northern Lakes. He'd gotten him the job at the firehouse and a room at the boardinghouse. From the social worker's notes and Cody's own comments to Braden, she knew the kid had had some developmental challenges. He was capable enough to drive and work, even if he wasn't as mature as other kids his age.

Stanley shook his head and timidly murmured, "It's too dangerous…"

"It certainly has been lately," she agreed, "with that arsonist on the loose."

He shuddered. "I know…"

"You were in danger yourself," she said, "when the boardinghouse caught fire."

"Annie and Cody saved me."

"You were brave," she praised him. "To go back into the burning house to rescue the dog." Had he not realized the dog had been inside when he'd set the fire?

Or had he intended to hurt the animal and then changed his mind?

It was so hard to imagine this sweet kid wanting to hurt anyone. But she couldn't let that stop her from doing her job.

Stanley's face flushed and he stared down at the table, as if unable to meet her eyes. "I'm not brave at all."

"That took a lot of guts," she said. "To go back into that house."

"Back in?" he asked. "I just drove up when Serena was getting Mrs. G and Mr. S out of the house."

"Mrs. G and Mr. S?" She knew from the report that Mrs. Gulliver and Mr. Stehouwer were elderly boarders who'd lived in the house before Serena's mother had passed away the year before. But she wanted to hear what Stanley thought of them, to find out if he would have put them in danger.

"They're great," he said. And he looked up now, his brown eyes warm with affection. "They live in an assisted-living center now—together." He smiled.

"It was good nothing happened to them."

A ragged breath escaped. "Yeah…"

"So if you saw Serena outside with them, why did you go inside?" she asked.

"I heard Annie barking," he said with another shudder. "I don't know if I ever heard her bark before that. She sounded scared—like she was trapped."

He sounded so earnest, so upset, that compassion warmed Sam's heart. "You rescued her."

"No," he said. "I tried, but I would have died if Cody hadn't gotten back when he did…"

"From the wildfire out West," she said. "The Hotshots had just returned to Northern Lakes when the fire started." While Braden had been with Wyatt, Dawson and Cody at the firehouse, the other members of the team were unaccounted for. It could have been one of them or it could have been Stanley. He was almost an honorary Hotshot.

He tensed now, as if he heard an accusation in her words. She'd been careful to put him at ease.

She continued, "None of them can help me figure out who's responsible for the fires. I need your help, Stanley."

His face turned a deeper shade of red now. And he nervously shook his head. "Why—why would you think I know anything about the fires?"

"You've been here for all of them," she said.

He met her gaze now, his eyes wide with shock and fear. "You think I started them?"

She'd thought he was slow. At least that was what the social worker's file on him had claimed—slow learner, slow reader, slow thinker…

But he'd picked up quickly on where she was heading with her questions. Maybe everyone—her and Braden included—had underestimated sweet Stanley.

"I'm just saying you've been around for every fire,"

she said. And without an alibi. Of course no one had asked him for an alibi because no one had suspected Stanley.

Until now...

Braden had suspected Stanley, but he hadn't been able to bring himself to question him. He'd wanted to protect him—even if he was the one responsible. Yeah, Stanley was one of his team members, and he considered him family.

"So that makes me guilty?" Stanley asked, his voice rising with panic.

"No," she said. "That means you could have seen something to help us find out who's guilty."

He shook his head.

"You've been around for every fire," she repeated. "You must have seen something."

"No, no," he said, as he jumped up from the table. "You're not going to pin this on me."

She stood up, too, and moved toward the door to stop him from running out. "Of course not," she assured him. "Nobody's going to pin anything on you that you didn't do."

"But *you* think I did it!" he said, and the accusation was in his voice now. "*You* think I'm guilty."

She hadn't moved quickly enough. He shoved past her and ran out the door. She stumbled back but couldn't regain her feet before she landed on the floor. Her breath escaped in a whoosh. His footsteps pounded down the stairs.

She needed to get up—needed to chase after him. But she suspected it would get her nowhere. He wasn't going to tell her any more than he already had. Questioning him had done no good. She still had no idea if he was guilty or innocent.

BRADEN HEARD THE running footsteps and planted himself at the bottom of the concrete stairwell. "What's wrong?" he asked as the kid barreled down the steps.

Stanley drew up short, tears streaming down his face.

Guilt squeezed Braden's heart. Maybe he shouldn't have brought Stanley to Sam's attention. But he couldn't have risked anyone else getting hurt. He couldn't have risked *her* getting hurt.

"She—she thinks I'm guilty," Stanley stammered nervously.

Was he scared because he was guilty or because he wasn't? Braden studied his face, trying to decipher the emotions moving across it. Then he saw the shock.

"You think I'm guilty, too!" Stanley exclaimed.

Braden reached out to grab his shoulders, but the teenager wriggled away and ran from the firehouse. Moments later an engine roared and tires squealed as he raced away in his old Pontiac.

Cody had bought him the car, just like he'd gotten him the job. He'd done so much for the teenager he clearly considered to be like a younger brother. Why would Stanley have responded to all that by trying to kill Cody? By trying to kill the woman Cody loved?

Braden lowered his head and uttered a heavy sigh. A small hand squeezed his shoulder, and a soft voice murmured, "I'm sorry."

He turned toward Sam. She looked as miserable as he felt. "Was it like kicking a puppy?"

"Yeah," she said with a heavy sigh of her own. "But that puppy had the most means and opportunity."

"But no motive," Braden said. "The kid wouldn't hurt a fly—no matter how much he's been hurt." And Braden had just caused him pain again. "He couldn't even leave

Annie at the pound when we told him to. He was worried that no one would adopt her and she'd be put down."

"Like no one had adopted him…"

"You read his file," Braden surmised. He sure had—before he'd hired him.

"Other arsonists have had similarly unhappy childhoods," she said. "He's a viable suspect."

He shook his head. "No. I was wrong," he said. "I never should have brought up his name."

"You didn't," she reminded him, and she sounded a little irritated now—with him. "You were very careful not to."

He gestured toward the open overhead door. Stanley was long gone, though. "Because I didn't want this to happen," he said. "I didn't want to hurt him."

She smiled now and slid her hand down his arm. "You can't protect everyone," she said. "Especially the guilty. That might not have been hurt. That could have been fear that he's been discovered."

"Do you believe that?" he asked. "Do you really believe that sweet kid is guilty?"

She lifted her shoulders in a slight shrug. "He's around here more than anyone else is," she said. "He could have easily put that note on your desk and left those hay bales to burn in the garage."

The concrete was scorched black from where the fire had flared.

Stanley could have done those things. And Braden's stomach lurched with dread that he had. But he couldn't accept it was the kid. "That doesn't mean it's him."

"I don't want it to be him, either," she admitted. "And I haven't known him as long as you have."

He appreciated that she understood how special Stanley was. "Thank you," he said, and he touched her now, moving his hand from her shoulder down her arm to her hand.

They'd had sex a couple of times now, but they hadn't even held hands. Of course, they hadn't gone on a date, either. They hadn't sat together at a movie. Or stared at each other across a candlelit dinner table.

But that was because they weren't dating. Braden hadn't been out of the dating pool so long he didn't realize that. Sam wasn't his girlfriend. She was just his arson investigator.

Still, her fingers naturally entwined with his, just like they'd naturally moved together when they'd made love. He'd expected that the first time with a woman other than his wife would be awkward. He'd been married to Ami for three years and had dated her for two before their wedding, so it had been a while since he'd been with anyone but her.

Too bad the same hadn't been true for her.

He waited for the flash of pain and bitterness he usually felt when he thought about her betrayal. But he didn't feel it now.

He only felt the silkiness of Sam's skin and the heat of her touch. He'd never felt like this about his wife; it had never been as natural—as instinctive—with Ami as it was with Sam.

She squeezed his fingers. "Just because we don't want it to be him doesn't mean that it's not."

"No," he agreed. "But I can't see him hurting Cody and Serena. They're like his parents. He loves them so much."

"Like I said, I don't want it to be him, either," Sam said. "He's a sweet kid. But I can't be sure until we rule him out as a suspect."

"We'll rule him out," Braden said, and the heaviness

in his heart eased slightly, but he wasn't going to forgive himself any time soon. And he suspected Stanley wouldn't, either. How would he explain? How would he apologize?

"I hope we do," Sam said. Her hand slipped away from his, and her brow furrowed with thought. "But guilty or not, I think he knows something."

"What?"

"He's always around," she said. "Just like you pointed out. He was here when that note was left. He was here when the hay bales were set on fire."

"He said he wasn't," Braden reminded her. "He was walking Annie."

She tilted her head. "And you believe him?"

"What reason would he have to lie?"

"The same reason you do what you do," she said.

He opened his mouth to ask exactly what he did.

But she continued, "He's protecting someone."

The pressure was back on his chest, heavier than before. "No…"

"He's always around here," she said. "That's what made you consider him a suspect. He couldn't be around all the time like that and not have noticed something."

"And you think he would protect that person?" Braden asked.

She nodded. "If it's someone he knows, someone he cares about…"

"But this person is dangerous," Braden said. "He can't trust him."

"No, he can't," she agreed. "Especially now. The arsonist knows I'm in town—knows I'm investigating."

"And wants you to leave," Braden said, remembering the broken window and the note. *Or bad things will happen.*

"If the arsonist thinks Stanley might talk..." She trailed off, her beautiful face tense with concern.

"He's in danger," Braden said.

She nodded.

Braden had made the mistake of trusting someone he shouldn't have. He'd thought his mistake had forever cost him his heart. Now he wasn't so sure.

But he was sure that Stanley's mistake would cost him. Maybe his life...

13

SAM'S HEART BEAT QUICKLY. Maybe because she was afraid for Stanley. Maybe because she was in Braden's office again, working on the computer on his desk.

Braden was gone. He'd raced off to find Stanley. Hopefully he would get through to the kid. She suspected his chances were better alone than with her present. She had only been around for a week; she was a relative stranger to the teenager.

What did he know?

He hadn't been in town long when that first fire had happened. He'd already been working at the firehouse, though. So he'd met the entire Hotshot team. He knew all of them.

There were some volunteers as well who covered the firehouse when the Hotshots were out West. But she had already checked them out.

Most were older retirees. Fortunately the arsonist hadn't set any fires when they were covering for the Hotshots, or the entire town probably would have burned down. Or was Stanley working for one of the Hotshots? Owen James? Was Owen angry that his former classmate had passed him over for promotion, instead favoring Wyatt Andrews and Dawson Hess?

Had he manipulated Stanley into doing his dirty work for him? The kid was sweet and naive enough that it would be easy to coerce him.

She sighed and leaned her head down, tempted to pound it against the surface of the desk. But then she heard the noise, the footsteps padding across the concrete floor.

Had Stanley come back?

Or could it be the arsonist? He seemed to frequent the firehouse when no one was around. And maybe Stanley and the arsonist were one and the same. She couldn't take any chances. She reached for her purse and withdrew her gun. She'd just raised the barrel when the office door opened.

A man gasped and raised his hands. All the color drained from Owen James's face, leaving it stark but for the jagged scar on one cheek.

"What are you doing here?" she asked, her voice sharp as she steadied her grip on the Glock.

"I stopped by to talk to Braden."

"Talk to him?" Or hurt him?

Owen's dark eyes narrowed. "Yes, talk—about what's been going on…" His hands shaking, he gestured at the gun she still held, the barrel pointed at him. "Are you going to put that down?"

She wasn't so sure that she should. So she hesitated.

"I heard you got a note, too," he said. "So I understand why you would be a little nervous."

"Cautious," she corrected him. "Not nervous." She wasn't afraid of the arsonist; she was just determined to catch him. And it had less to do with her career now than it had to do with Braden—with making sure he was safe.

"How did you hear about the note?" she wondered. Because he'd smashed her window and put it in her car?

He shrugged. "Northern Lakes is a small town. I grew up here. I know everyone."

He was the local hero—for surviving his deployment, for acting as an EMT when he was back in town. Nobody would suspect him of being involved in the fires.

Nobody but her.

"Where is Braden?" he asked.

Did he really want to find Braden or just make certain she was alone? She shivered, but lowered the gun. She wasn't putting it back in her purse, though—not until he was gone. "He went to look for Stanley."

Owen chuckled. "What? Did that kid get lost chasing after his dog again?"

"I hope he's not lost," she murmured. Hopefully Braden had found him, protected him as he tried to protect everyone.

Owen raised a dark blond brow. "What's going on? Is the kid in trouble?" He seemed curious but not overly concerned. If he was working with Stanley, wouldn't he be worried that the kid had talked?

She intended to find out, so she said, "I questioned him today—"

"Stanley?" He sounded shocked, but then he lowered both brows and slowly nodded. "Stanley…"

"What?"

"It makes sense," he said. "He's always around here."

"But what's his motive?" she asked.

He shrugged shoulders, which were nearly as broad and muscular as Braden's. Every member of his Hotshot team was in excellent shape. Requiring that was another way for Braden to protect them—to make sure they were prepared to do their dangerous jobs. Her father prepared his smoke jumper teams the same way.

"I don't know what his motive could be," Owen said.

"Braden doesn't think he'd hurt anyone."

Owen smiled. "Braden always thinks the best of everyone."

Even his ex-wife.

"Yes, he does."

"It's just not realistic," Owen said. "There are bad people in the world—so many bad people."

"Stanley's just a kid."

"And kids don't do bad things?" Owen challenged her.

They did. Matthew Hamilton had when he'd destroyed his mother's boyfriend's property. But maybe that hadn't been such a bad thing if the guy was as nasty as he sounded.

"Why would Stanley?" she asked. "He doesn't seem like an angry kid."

"Sometimes he seems afraid," Owen said. And now his brow furrowed. "It reminds me..." His face grew pale again, and she could imagine what it reminded him of. Afghanistan. Iraq. Wherever he'd been deployed when he had gotten that horrible scar.

"When I was deployed with the Marines, those kids," he said, "over there. They didn't want to strap on those explosives. They didn't want to hurt anyone."

"Why did they?" she asked.

"They had been threatened," Owen said. "Most commonly, their families had been threatened. They were given no choice but to do bad things."

A chill raced down Sam's spine. She shivered in reaction. "Of course."

"But Stanley has no family," Owen pointed out.

"Yes, he does," Sam said. "He has the Hotshots." But

would he hurt one of them in order to protect the others? Would he hurt Braden?

She shouldn't have let him go off to look for the kid alone. It wasn't safe. Nowhere was safe for Braden until the arsonist was caught.

She shoved her gun back into her purse and slung the strap over her shoulder. Braden was out there with no protection.

"What's wrong?" Owen asked.

She didn't pause to explain. She just pushed past him and hurried out the door. She hoped she wouldn't be too late. She hoped that Braden was okay.

BRADEN BRACED HIMSELF for the blow. But while Cody had doubled his hands into fists, he didn't swing them. He just paced the front porch around Braden.

"How dare you let her interrogate that poor kid!" Cody exclaimed. "He just tore out of here in tears."

Braden hadn't seen Stanley's rusted Pontiac in the driveway. But it hadn't passed him, either.

Since the boardinghouse had burned down, Cody, Serena and Stanley had been staying at Wyatt's house in town, and Wyatt had moved in with his fiancée, Fiona. Wyatt's small house was on the side of the firehouse away from town. Stanley must have headed toward the forest, because he hadn't passed Braden.

So he'd stopped to talk to Cody, to see if he knew where the boy had gone.

"I don't care that she's Mack's daughter," Cody continued. "She doesn't know what the hell she's doing. You need to get her off this case."

"I kind of asked her to do it," Braden admitted.

Cody's mouth fell open, and he stared at him in shock. "How could you?"

"I had to," Braden said. "We have to stop the arsonist."

Now a gasp slipped through Cody's lips. "You can't seriously believe that Stanley is the arsonist."

"He fits the profile," Braden said. Like Sam, he had taken some profiling courses at Quantico. "He has the same kind of background—the rough childhood—so many serial arsonists have."

Cody's throat moved as if he were choking. Then his voice rasped, "So do I."

Braden reached out. But Cody flinched and stepped away from him. "I would never doubt you."

"You shouldn't have doubted Stanley, either," Cody said. "He would never hurt anyone."

Braden couldn't say the same anymore. He knew he'd hurt Stanley. And now he'd hurt Cody, too. Regret and guilt twisted his stomach into knots.

"Sam thinks Stanley knows something," Braden persisted. "That he's protecting someone."

Cody's brow furrowed. "*You* think he would protect the arsonist?"

Braden wondered about his question—until he noticed that Sam stood at the bottom of the steps leading up to the porch and Cody had asked her the question directly.

She stared up at Braden, a look of relief on her beautiful face. "You're okay," she murmured as if she'd been concerned about him.

He nodded. "Of course." Though he wouldn't have blamed Cody had he hit him. Braden actually might have felt better if he had. Maybe it would have eased his guilt a little.

"Who do you suspect?" Cody asked Sam.

"What about Matthew Hamilton?" Sam asked as she joined them on the porch. "Would Stanley protect him? Or let him bully or coerce him?"

At the mention of the teenager's name, Cody glared at her. "You had no right to talk to Stanley without a lawyer."

She shrugged. "He didn't want one."

"He's not mature enough to make that decision on his own," Cody insisted.

"He's eighteen."

"Why are you asking about Matt again?" Braden interrupted them.

"Because his name has come up a couple of times," Sam said. "And Stanley might try to protect him if he thinks they're friends."

Cody sucked in a breath. "Matt? No way. He's Fiona's brother. He's like Wyatt's little brother."

"He was really upset when he didn't get a position with the US Forest Service fire department," Sam replied.

Braden regretted now making note of that in his investigation. But he'd followed up. He reminded her of what he'd told her the last time she'd brought up the twenty-year-old. "He has an alibi."

"His *mother* alibied him for the fires," Sam said.

Cody snorted derisively. "His mother?"

"I can't speak personally about mothers," Sam said. "But I have a dad who would do anything to protect his kids."

Cody studied Sam with renewed admiration. "Yeah, I've heard about those kind of parents." But he hadn't had them. The people who'd adopted him had returned him after a few years, claiming he'd put a stress on their marriage.

Braden was fortunate his parents had been loving and supportive. They still were, even though they'd moved out West. He visited whenever he had time when he was working fires out there. And they called often—too much when he'd been going through his divorce. Everybody had been trying to get him to talk, when he'd just wanted to forget about it.

"So Matt's off the hook because of his mother, and Stanley's SOL?" Cody asked defensively.

"Matthew doesn't just have a mother who would do anything for him," Braden said—though he couldn't deny that Mandy would. She had felt terrible that her son had gotten in trouble all those years ago because of her bad choices in men. She'd even sworn him and Wyatt to secrecy, so they wouldn't tell Fiona. Her relationship with her daughter was shaky at best. "He has security footage from the hotel where she works. It's time-stamped, so it supports the alibi she gave him."

Cody pushed a shaky hand over his short blond hair. "I want to be happy for Matt and Fiona. But I want you to find who's really responsible so you can leave Stanley alone."

"We need to find Stanley," Braden said.

"To arrest him?" Serena asked the question as she joined them on the porch. The black-haired beauty's usually tanned complexion had paled with fear.

Braden shook his head and assured her, "Neither Sam nor I think he's responsible, but we're concerned he might know who is." And that knowledge would put him in danger.

The arsonist had already threatened Sam, who didn't know who he was. What would he do to someone who did? What would he do to that trusting kid?

Serena held out a note, and her fingers were trembling. "I just found this in his room." She turned to Cody. "He took *all* his stuff and Annie, too."

Braden took the note from her. And Cody took Serena, closing his arms around her as she clung to him.

Sam stepped close to Braden's side and peered around him at the paper in his hand. She sucked in a breath, and he turned to her. But her attention was on the paper, so he looked down at it, too.

A breath escaped his lips in a gasp. The blocky handwriting matched the notes the arsonist had been leaving. But the handwriting was the only thing that matched. This was no threat. It was two simple words: **I'M SORRY**.

"I know what this looks like," Cody said, as he glanced at the note, too. "But it's not that. Stanley could never hurt anyone."

Braden didn't know what to think anymore. He had misjudged people close to him before. He'd misjudged Ami for damn certain. And if he believed Sam, there might be someone else on his team he had misjudged—someone who was a danger to everyone else if those previous accidents hadn't really been accidents.

But he struggled to believe Stanley could have acted alone. The kid just didn't have it in him to be a criminal mastermind, and the arsonist was smart or he would have been caught before now.

Usually arsonists didn't work in pairs; he knew that as well as Sam did. But maybe someone had used Stanley—for access to the firehouse and to write those notes. So Stanley was still in danger—just like everyone else.

14

SAM WAS MISSING SOMETHING. And not just Braden. She was missing him, too. But she was missing something about the arsonist. When she'd interviewed Stanley, she had all but ruled him out as a suspect. Like Braden, she believed he wouldn't be capable of hurting anyone—at least, she'd wanted to believe that.

Had she been wrong?

She needed to know. So she walked into Braden's office. Glancing at his desk, she realized what else she needed: him. He'd made her feel things she hadn't felt before. She wanted to feel them again—wanted to feel *him* again.

He looked up, and his dark eyes brightened. "You're still here."

"You thought I left town?" she asked. It had only been a few hours since she'd parted ways with him at Cody Mallehan's house.

He nodded. "I figured you'd take that note as confirmation Stanley's the arsonist and close the case."

She sighed. "The handwriting matches the others pretty closely." She had sent the note off to the same state police lab that had processed the others to confirm they'd been written by the same person.

She settled into the chair in front of his desk. "I wondered why Avery got the threatening notes and now you, but Cody and Serena received nothing."

"Because they would have recognized the handwriting," Braden said, but then he shook his head. "It still doesn't make sense, though. Stanley nearly died in that fire—trying to get his dog out. Serena nearly died trying to rescue them." He shuddered now, as if recalling how close it had been.

Sam had seen the photos. She knew that it had been a miracle anyone had survived that fire.

"He wouldn't have put himself in danger like that if he was the arsonist," Braden continued. "And he wouldn't have hurt Cody and Serena. He loves them."

"He said he was sorry." Sam reminded him of the kid's last note. And for that very reason alone, she doubted he was really the arsonist. Usually the culprit was defensive and full of excuses, never taking responsibility for what they'd done, instead blaming it on a bad childhood—on anything and anyone else. They never apologized.

She shook her head now, too. "No, Stanley is not the arsonist. He might have written those notes, but he didn't set the fires."

"If he wrote the notes for the arsonist, he definitely knows who he is," Braden said.

"We need to find him," she said.

"Cody and Serena are looking for him," Braden said. "Everyone else is out helping them."

"I'm not sure that's the best idea," she said. "One of them could be the arsonist. You can't trust anybody."

"I learned that the hard way once," Braden remarked.

"With your ex-wife..." She trailed off. "You don't think she would...?"

"Use Stanley?" He shook his head. "No."

"You don't think a woman can be an arsonist?"

His mouth curved into a grin. "You are determined to believe I'm a chauvinist."

"It has nothing to do with chauvinism," she said. She was determined to consider his ex a suspect. Sam wasn't sure why it bothered her so much that this woman had cheated on Braden and hurt him. She also worried he might still be hung up on her. It seemed as if Ami had no problem getting whatever man she wanted, whether he was married or not. What would happen if she went after Braden again?

Was Ami a mistake he would make again? Or had he learned his lesson like she had with Chad and Blake? She would never date men like either of them again. Not that she had time to date anyone right now—not until she had firmly established herself as the best arson investigator in the US Forest Service.

So it shouldn't matter to her if Braden did go back to his ex. It wasn't like she wanted a future with him. She didn't want a future with anyone right now.

She smiled and said, "I was just giving you a hard time."

Something flickered in his eyes, like a match in the dark. "Oh, believe me, you do."

She couldn't miss the innuendo in his voice. Nor did she want to. She wanted him too much. "Braden..."

BRADEN WANTED SAM AGAIN. On the desk. In the conference room. Hell, even on a bed. He didn't care where; he just had to have her. When he'd thought she might have left town...

His stomach sank again like it had when he'd first considered she could be gone. If he hadn't been able to kiss her again...

Or touch her. Or be with her. But eventually she would leave. When she did, he wanted to be able to say goodbye, though. "When I thought you left without saying goodbye..."

She sucked in a breath. "I wouldn't."

He stood up so quickly his chair fell back as he moved toward her.

She stood, too, raised her arm and pressed her hand against his chest, holding him back. "I wouldn't leave without saying goodbye," she assured him.

But she would leave. They both knew that. Northern Lakes had never had an arsonist before and they were unlikely to have one again. Once she caught this guy, she'd have no reason to ever return to the northeastern Michigan town.

No reason...

She moved her hand from his chest, slid it up to his neck and pulled his head down toward hers. She kissed him softly, pressing her lips to his.

It was a tender kiss, the first tender one they'd shared. But then their passion ignited like the match on the gasoline-soaked hay. Her fingers clutched at his hair.

He reached down and cupped her butt in his hands and lifted her up. She locked her legs around his waist. But he moved her higher. Then he tugged off her sweater and unhooked her bra. He kissed her breasts, flicking his tongue across her tightened nipples.

She moaned and arched back.

He felt the heat of her through his shirt and her pants. He wanted nothing between them.

She must have felt the same because she wriggled

down. As she slid over his groin, his cock throbbed and pulsed, begging to be freed. Her fingers tugged on his zipper tab, pulling it down to free him.

Her skin silky, she stroked her fingers up and down the length of him. He groaned and struggled for control. But she tested it. Dropping to her knees, she replaced her fingers with her mouth. She slid her lips up and down like she had her hand. Her tongue circled around him, lapping at him.

Heat flooded his body as tension filled him. He wanted to just let go—to just come. But he couldn't without pleasing her first. He had to make sure he made her happy.

He reached out and stroked his fingers through her silky hair. "Sam..."

She looked up at him as she slid her mouth to the tip of his cock. And she watched his face as she sucked on him.

He groaned. "I need you now!"

But first he had to make sure she was ready. He tugged her to her feet. His fingers trembled as he fumbled with the snap and zipper of her pants. Then he pushed them down along with her panties and stroked his fingers over her. He found her wet and hot and ready for him.

As he slid his finger inside her, she whimpered and arched against his hand. "Braden..."

He kissed her deeply, moving his lips back and forth over hers. She opened her mouth, inviting him inside, but she didn't wait for him. The tip of her tongue stroked over his bottom lip. Then her teeth nipped at it.

He groaned again. Straining for control, he pulled away from her, just long enough to find a condom and sheathe himself. Then he lifted her again.

She cradled his cock in her hand and guided him toward her core. As she locked her legs around his waist, she took him deeply inside her.

This time he settled his ass onto the edge of his desk, which was cold beneath his bare skin. He braced himself against the surface as she moved up and down. His cock slid in and nearly out as she raised and lowered herself.

The sensation of her inner muscles squeezing him almost drove him out of his mind. His every muscle tensed as pressure built inside him. Cupping as much of her full breasts as he could in his hands, he rubbed his thumbs over her tightened nipples.

She nipped at his shoulder with her teeth and raked her short nails down his back. Seemingly as desperate for release as he was, she moved frantically against him.

He moved his hands from her breasts to her hips, gripping the curves in his hands. He helped her move as he thrust his hips up.

Her body tensed, those inner muscles clutching him as she came. His name left her lips on a keening moan.

He wasn't sure if he'd ever pleased anyone like he seemed to please her. But then the feeling was mutual. His self-control snapped, and he pumped hard and fast until the powerful orgasm claimed him. It overwhelmed him with its intensity.

She shifted against him, as if trying to wriggle free. But he held her for just a moment before disengaging. He cleaned up and dressed quickly in case anyone came back to the firehouse.

How had he lost focus like that? How had he managed to forget everything but her? Because he'd thought he'd lost her...

What would he do when she was really gone? Maybe it wasn't so hard to imagine. He didn't really have her now. She had straightened her clothes, but her head was down, as if she couldn't meet his gaze.

Was she embarrassed? He was the one who'd lost control—who always lost control with her—even though he hadn't wanted to get involved with her, hadn't wanted to put her in danger.

Now he didn't want her to go. He stepped closer and slid his fingers under her chin, tipping it up so he could see into her beautiful blue eyes.

"So you're staying?" Braden asked her, needing that reassurance.

She nodded quickly, knocking his hand away. "Until we find Stanley and can confirm whether or not he acted alone."

"Of course."

The investigation was still her only reason for being in Northern Lakes. She wasn't staying because of him.

Braden knew that, but still he felt a twinge of disappointment. She'd made it clear she didn't want a relationship with him. And he'd felt the same way. Hell, he hadn't even been divorced that long. Getting serious about anyone would be a mistake—at least that's what he'd been telling himself.

But now he could admit he wanted more than just to find the arsonist. Or Stanley.

He wanted Sam—not just for sex but for so much more. Despite how many times she'd warned him she wasn't staying, he'd fallen for her.

He'd fallen fully, completely in love with Sam McRooney. When she left, and she would, he would find out how it felt for his heart to really break. He hoped he could survive the pain.

15

THE MINUTE SAM had said she would stay until they found Stanley, Braden had suggested joining the search for him. Did he want her gone that badly? Just moments before he'd wanted her—desperately so.

She glanced over at his face. He was staring intently through the windshield, his hands tightly gripping the steering wheel of his US Forest Service pickup truck. Unlike Sam's rental, it was a four-wheel drive, so it could take them wherever they needed to go. Hopefully, Stanley was still in Northern Lakes.

Of course Braden wanted to find the kid. He felt responsible for him, just like he felt responsible for everyone and everything. He wanted to protect him.

But she wasn't entirely sure Stanley needed protection. Maybe he *had* acted alone. Maybe he wasn't the sweet kid they'd all believed he was.

She reached across the console and slid her fingers along Braden's arm. The muscles tensed beneath her touch. "It's not your fault, you know."

He glanced over at her. "What?"

"Stanley," she said. "What else do you think is your fault?"

He shook his head. "It's just hard for me to believe Stanley is really involved."

"Not that hard," she said, "or you wouldn't have pointed him out to me."

He sighed. "I was looking at who had the opportunity. I couldn't let myself consider he might really be the arsonist."

"Was that the same as the situation with your ex?" she asked. "Did you suspect, but then didn't want to admit she was capable of cheating?"

He glanced over at her again, his dark eyes wide with surprise. After a long moment, he finally replied, "Maybe."

"Owen says that you always look for the best in everyone."

"He thinks Stanley did it?"

"He thinks he's capable," she admitted. Was that because he'd manipulated Stanley into working with him? Or was Ethan Sommerly the one who'd done that? She'd found out the reclusive Hotshot came from a rich family. He could have bought Stanley's help.

Braden's hands gripped the wheel tighter. So tight, she wondered if it might snap. Then he eased his grasp. "After what he's been through, Owen only sees the worst in people."

"Not in you," she said. "Your team loves you." And while it made the most sense for the arsonist to be one of them, she struggled to believe it could be. Maybe Gingrich *had* tampered with the dash-cam video.

She hoped he had.

"Not anymore," he said. "Cody is furious with me."

"He's furious with me." She was used to that, though. Nobody liked her questioning a friend or family member.

Nobody wanted to believe anyone they knew was actually capable of committing a crime.

She squeezed Braden's arm. "We'll find him."

He glanced at her, and now he looked skeptical. "He could be anywhere," he said. "He could be far from Northern Lakes by now."

"He could be…" But somehow she doubted that. "He's not like other suspects, though, who might seek out family members to help them elude authorities." That was how she'd tracked down previous suspects, at the homes of family or friends.

Braden sighed. "No, Stanley really has no place to go." He glanced across at her. "Not like you."

"Me?"

"You have your place in DC," he said. "Your father's in Washington. Where are your brothers?"

"I'm not sure I could go to my brothers," she said. "If I was in trouble, they'd probably be the first to turn me in." Despite the stunts they'd pulled when they were younger, they were all about doing the right thing now. And they'd always loved getting her in trouble since it had happened so rarely. They'd always complained she was their father's favorite. "Trick is in Idaho. Rand works with Mack in Washington. And…"

When she trailed off, he prodded her. "Did you forget one?"

"No," she said. "I just don't know where Mack is."

He glanced at her again, his brow furrowed. "Washington—you just said that."

"No, my brother Mack," she explained. "I don't know where he is."

"You haven't heard from him?"

"He calls. We text," she said. "I'm just not sure where he's stationed right now." But that was Mackie. He was fiercely independent—like her. He didn't want to be tied down to one location. Neither did she.

But she wasn't sure how easy it would be for her to leave once she caught the arsonist. Not that she'd become particularly attached to Northern Lakes. Her conflicted feelings were entirely due to Braden Zimmer. She'd never met a more impressive man.

He wouldn't be easy for her to leave or forget once she was gone. But she had to leave. She loved her job. And she had no intention of giving it up. Her mom had done that—given up her career to marry Mack and have a family. But she must have resented that sacrifice enough that she hadn't been able to stay.

Just like Sam knew she couldn't stay, either. But she wouldn't make the mistake her mother had. She wouldn't try to be something she wasn't.

SAM HAD FALLEN curiously quiet next to him, and her hand had slipped away from his arm. Braden missed her touch. Missed her conversation…

He glanced over at her, but she was turned away from him, looking out the passenger's window. "Do you see anything?" he asked, just to get her to talk.

She shook her head to indicate she hadn't. But then he did. The car was parked on Braden's side of the street—near the campsite where the Boy Scouts had nearly been killed in that very first fire.

He pressed on the brakes. And Sam whirled toward him. "Why are you—" Then she saw the rusted Pontiac, too. "He didn't leave."

"He had no place else to go," Braden reminded her. He parked the truck in front of the car. Of course Stanley could just back up and drive around him. The grass was already matted down behind the car. But Braden didn't see anyone inside it.

He twisted his key in the ignition, turning off the engine. And he listened. Somewhere in the distance a dog barked. "Annie," he murmured. But he'd never actually heard the overgrown puppy bark. He wouldn't have even believed she was capable if Cody and Stanley hadn't told him how frantically she'd been barking in that burning boardinghouse.

Her bark sounded frantic now. He threw open the driver's door and stepped out. Sam was at his side within seconds, her gun drawn.

And he realized why she'd insisted on coming with him. To protect him.

He was used to being the protector—the boss, the one who looked out for everyone else. He wasn't used to having someone look out for him. And hell, maybe he was a chauvinist because it was especially weird to have a woman—one so petite and beautiful—protecting him. The caveman in him wanted to be the one shielding her.

But Sam was strong and independent. She didn't need anyone. She didn't want anyone or anything but to do her job. She hurried ahead, then stopped and turned back to him. "Where is the dog?"

He cocked his head and listened now, trying to determine from which direction Annie's barking was coming. It seemed to carry throughout the forest.

"Is that even Annie?" Sam asked, her voice soft as if afraid they might be overheard. Her grasp was tight on her gun.

He was glad that she had it—to protect herself. Not that he thought Stanley was actually dangerous...

But the sun was beginning to set, casting shadows in the woods as he headed off in the direction the barking seemed to come from. Braden wasn't sure it was only Stanley and Annie they would find. There was an urgency to the dog's barking.

"That's her," he said. He instinctively knew it was Annie. Braden lifted his head and sniffed the air. But he caught no trace of smoke. Annie wasn't barking over a fire this time—not like she had before. And he didn't smell gasoline.

"Are we heading in the right direction?" Sam asked.

The barking was so loud and frantic it seemed to come from everywhere as it echoed through trees and ravines. Braden suspected they'd started walking in circles trying to follow the sound.

So he called out, "Annie! Annie!"

"Shh," Sam cautioned him as she swung her gun around, pointing the barrel into looming shadows. "He'll know we're here."

He wasn't sure who she was talking about—Stanley or the arsonist. Braden still couldn't believe they were one and the same.

"You have a gun," Braden said. "Stanley doesn't."

"I'm not worried about Stanley," she said. So she didn't believe he'd acted alone.

"I am," he said. Because the dog sounded scared. "Annie!"

The barking ceased.

"What if the arsonist is here?"

"I only saw Stanley's car," he said, but then remembered the grass behind the Pontiac had been matted down. Something must have been parked there not long before they arrived.

"Annie!" Sam yelled for the dog now, then gasped at the sound of twigs snapping and brush rustling. She swung her barrel around—as the dog burst through the underbrush and ran toward them.

Annie, her hair tangled and matted with dirt and briars, planted her paws on Braden's chest and licked his chin. But her greeting was brief. She dropped back to the ground and whirled around—heading back from where she came.

"I think she wants us to follow her," Sam mused.

"She pisses in my office but acts like Lassie," he murmured. "Who knew?"

The branches rattled as the dog turned back. She barked as if telling them to hurry. Braden quickened his step, rushing after her. "We're coming."

But the dog was moving fast. He lost sight of her as the trees and underbrush thickened. His foot slipped on some slick earth, and his leg moved forward—over an embankment. He reached out, grabbing for branches to stop himself from falling into the steep ravine.

Small hands grabbed at his shoulders, clutching him. "Are you okay?" Sam asked.

"Yes," he said. "But where did Annie go?"

The dog pushed through the branches again as she came up from the ravine. She straddled him, licking his face and whimpering. She desperately wanted him to follow her.

And Braden felt sick as he realized why. Stanley was in the ravine. "He's down there."

"Do you see him?" Sam asked as she crept closer to the edge and peered down into the brush. She dropped her gun into her purse and strapped the bag across her body. To go down into the ravine, she would need both hands.

"No," Braden admitted. But it was clearly where Annie wanted him to go. She crashed through the brush again as she headed down the steep side of the ravine.

Braden followed, his feet slipping on the dirt the dog had loosened while branches slapped him and briars tugged at his pants.

Like the barking, the sound of snapping twigs and branches filled the air around him now—from Annie in front and Sam behind. "Don't come down here," he called after her. But it was too late.

She skidded down the hill and fell against his back. He caught and steadied her despite his own balance being so precarious.

Holding her with one hand, he navigated branches and tree trunks as they slowly descended to the bottom of the ravine. But he still didn't see Stanley or the dog. Then Annie barked, drawing his attention to the other slope.

Braden's heart lurched in his chest as he caught sight of the body lying broken among the brush. He jumped across the trickle of a stream at the bottom and rushed over to Stanley.

The dog already lay next to him, licking the boy's pale face and whining. Blood matted Stanley's curls and trickled from a deep gash on his head. One of his arms lay at an odd angle, and more blood oozed where a bone had broken through the skin.

"Call 911!" Braden shouted as he knelt beside the kid and searched for a pulse on his neck.

It throbbed weakly beneath his fingertips. "He's alive but just barely!"

Annie licked his hand as if she'd understood—as if she thought Braden could save him. But he wasn't sure it would be possible to save Stanley. He looked so deathly pale.

Sam had pulled her phone from her purse but she held it up. "I don't have a signal." She turned and scrambled back up the bank. "I'll keep trying."

"Go back to the truck," Braden told her. "There's a radio in it. Hit the button and ask for Owen."

She paused and looked back at him and the boy as if she didn't want to leave them. "Did he fall?" she asked.

Maybe Owen could use that information when she called. So Braden looked around, but he didn't see any telltale marks coming down the bank. What he did see was a baseball-bat-sized tree limb lying next to him, with blood and hair stuck to the bark in a few different spots. He doubted the kid had fallen on it so precisely. No. Someone had taken a swing at him.

Braden shook his head. "I think someone hit him." Hard. And more than once. They'd wanted to kill him.

Sam looked around the woods as if she would be able to see a killer among all the trees and brush. "You should take my gun," she said.

"You keep it." He would rather she had protection when she went back through the woods alone. "Get to the truck. Get help!"

She nodded and scrambled back up the bank. She must have known Braden wouldn't need a gun if whoever had done this to Stanley came back.

He would take the son of a bitch out with his bare hands. Hell, he hoped he came back.

16

SAM STOOD ALONE in a corner of the hospital waiting room while the Huron Hotshots stood together, united against a common threat. But this was no fire. This was so much worse.

The county hospital wasn't very big, so neither was the waiting room. But it was quite homey, with oak wainscoting and plaid wallpaper. Despite the warmth of the room, Sam felt cold. What she'd seen—that poor broken kid—had chilled her to her soul.

What kind of monster could've hurt him like that?

Of course, when she'd been a firefighter and certainly as an arson investigator, she'd seen worse. It never got any easier, though. Maybe her dad was right; maybe she just wasn't tough enough.

Yet. But she would be.

The door to the waiting room opened and a gray-haired doctor joined them. "Who's the family for John Smith?" he asked.

Everyone looked blankly at one another except for Cody, who said, "Stanley's legal name is John Smith."

"Are you his next of kin?" the doctor asked Cody.

Sam's heart rate quickened with fear. Was the doctor

looking for the next of kin to give them bad news? Had the boy not survived?

Cody and Serena stepped forward; the blond man had his arm wrapped comfortingly around the black-haired woman's shoulders. But she trembled uncontrollably, anyway. "We're his family," Cody said.

"Who are you to him?" the doctor asked. "Brother? Sister?"

"He's like my brother."

"I can only speak to his next of kin," the doctor said.

A cry slipped through Serena's lips as Sam's mouth fell open, too. The same horrible thought had just occurred to Ms. Beaumont. Serena asked, "Didn't he make it?"

The doctor hesitated.

"He has no family," Cody said. "He's an orphan. He's been living with me and Serena. We are the only family he has."

The doctor glanced around as though worried the privacy police might arrest him if he spoke out of turn. "I can't talk to you about his medical condition."

If he hadn't survived, would the doctor have mentioned his condition? He had to be alive.

Cody must have thought so, too, because he asked, "What happened to him? What are his injuries?"

Sam had advised Braden to say nothing to the others about what they thought had happened. She wanted to flush out the arsonist, who had to be Stanley's attacker.

"He took quite a fall," the doctor said.

Sam held in a derisive snort. That had been no fall.

"I really can't say any more about his condition," the doctor said, "until I have authorization from a family member or durable power of attorney for him."

Another door opened, this one from the hall into the

waiting room. Owen James met the doctor's gaze and nodded. The doctor slipped back through the door to the surgical area.

"What the hell's going on?" Cody demanded to know, his voice cracking with emotion. "Where'd he go?"

Owen stepped forward and put one hand on Cody's shoulder and the other on Serena's. Everyone else gathered around behind them to listen. Even Sam crept closer. "Dr. Burns can't tell you what I will," he said.

"Is Stanley going to be okay?" Serena fearfully asked. "That's all I need to know."

Sam needed to know so much more—like who the hell had done that to the kid. She'd seen that bloodied branch. She'd had the state police collect it as evidence.

The waiting room was so silent despite the number of people filling it that everyone must have been holding their breaths. There was a collective expulsion of air when Owen said, "He's alive. And we have reason to be hopeful."

Serena turned fully into Cody's arms, clinging to him as she cried. "He's alive..."

But Cody was still tense. "How bad is it, Owen?"

Owen drew in an unsteady breath. "They set his broken arm and his wrist."

"What about his head?" Braden asked the question, his voice gruff.

Sam wanted to be next to him, clinging to him like Serena clung to Cody. But he wasn't hers for comfort or to comfort. Their only relationship was professional—except for those couple of slips. But they'd just been slips. Ones they couldn't repeat.

"His skull is cracked," Owen said. "They put in a plate with screws. He's in a medically induced coma because of the swelling on his brain."

Tears streaked from Serena's dark eyes. "How long will he be in that?" she asked, her voice tremulous with concern.

Owen shrugged. "It all depends on how much swelling there is. He took a few hard blows."

"Blows?" Serena gasped, and now anger surged in her dark eyes. "I thought he fell! Who did that to him? Who hurt him?"

They all turned from Owen to Braden now. They knew he'd found him. He glanced at Sam, and she instantly knew he was going to ignore her request. He was going to reveal too much. But given how upset everyone was, she could hardly blame him. "Someone may have tried to make it look like he fell, but I think Annie grabbed the weapon before he could hide it. Or hit Stanley with it again."

Sam had noticed the gouges in the branch. Annie's teeth.

"That damn dog," Cody murmured, and a couple of tears slipped from his eyes. "Is she all right?"

"She led us to him," Braden said. "She's fine. One of the troopers took her back to the firehouse for the night."

"I hope she got a piece of the son of a bitch!" Cody cursed. "Who the hell did this to him?"

Braden grabbed his shoulder and assured him, "We'll find out. We'll find him."

But Cody pulled away.

And a twinge of regret struck Sam's heart. She felt this was her fault—that she'd caused the rift between Braden and his team. But she'd only been doing her job.

Her job had nearly gotten a young man killed, though. If only she could have questioned him without him getting so upset…

If only she could have found a way to get him to trust her, to tell her everything he knew...

Whatever he knew had nearly gotten him killed. She'd missed something. She was also missing someone—someone besides Braden this time. All of the Hotshots were talking at once, asking questions, demanding answers.

Before they could turn toward her, she slipped unnoticed into the hall. Her hand shook as she pulled her cell phone from her purse. There was no signal in the hospital, so she had to step outside to where a handful of visitors and staff were smoking. She walked downwind from them and hit one of her contacts.

"Sammi, are you all right?" her father anxiously asked.

She closed her eyes as emotion overwhelmed her. And she saw that kid with all the blood matted in his hair and running down his face—his thin body at such odd angles. It never got any easier.

"Sammi!" Mack's voice cracked with fear now.

"Daddy," she said.

"What's wrong?" he asked. "What's going on? Do you need me to come to Northern Lakes? I can fly over in a few hours."

He would—if she needed him. But even though she'd called him, she realized he wasn't the man she needed right now. She needed Braden. But his team needed him more.

She sucked in a deep breath. No. She didn't need him. She didn't need her father, either. She was as tough as her brothers—as independent. "No, no," she said. "I'm fine. You don't need to come here."

"Did you catch the arsonist then?"

She let all her frustration bubble up when she sharply replied, "No."

Mack chuckled. "That's why you're upset."

"That's part of it," she said.

"Braden? Is he giving you trouble?"

"Trouble?" He'd been giving her mind-blowing pleasure. But her heart was troubled. "No. It's the arsonist."

"You said not catching him is only part of it," Mack reminded her. "It's Braden. Did you ignore my warning about his messy divorce? He's not ready for a relationship with anyone."

"Neither am I," she insisted. "I'm focused on my career—on this case. The arsonist just hurt a kid, Dad."

He cursed. "I'm sorry, baby. You'll catch him."

"I have to—before he hurts anyone else." Like Braden. And because Braden was at risk of winding up like poor Stanley, she buried her pride. She didn't care what her father thought now, didn't care if he thought she couldn't do her job. She needed his help—needed his legendary judgment. She hated to but she had to admit, "I know I'm missing something. I've gone over and over the reports from every fire but I can't see it."

"That's because you're reading other people's reports," he said. "You're missing it because they missed it. You need to start over—act like you're the only one who worked the case."

She opened her eyes and felt as if she could see clearly now. "You're right."

"Your old man knows more than you think."

She chuckled now. "I know that."

"Then be careful, Sammi baby."

"I won't let the arsonist get me," she promised him.

"I was talking about Braden Zimmer," he said. "Be careful you don't fall for him."

Her breath whooshed out as she realized she already had fallen for Braden.

WHERE THE HELL had Sam gone? Braden hadn't noticed when she slipped out of the waiting room. But he couldn't blame her—not like everyone else was. They were blaming him, too, holding him responsible for bringing Sam in to investigate. She'd only been doing her job. They needed to be reminded of that, but the hospital waiting room wasn't the place to hold a team meeting.

He would do that another time, after Stanley's condition improved. Then he would remind them they needed to stop the arsonist—no matter who he was. But it wasn't Stanley. The kid hadn't hit himself in the head.

Braden wanted to hold vigil with his team in the waiting room. But that wouldn't catch the arsonist. Was that why Sam had left? Had she realized who was responsible and left to apprehend him on her own?

Sure, she had a gun. She was certainly better prepared to confront the arsonist than Stanley had been. But a line had been crossed now. Until tonight, the arsonist hadn't really hurt anyone. He had tried, but all of his potential victims had escaped his fires unharmed. Once that line had been crossed, it couldn't be uncrossed. The arsonist was far more dangerous than he'd ever been.

Sam was smart and strong and resourceful. But she wasn't indestructible. He had to find her and make sure she hadn't taken on the arsonist alone. He hurried out of the waiting room into the hall.

But the door opened behind him and a deep voice called out, "I need to talk to you."

Even before he turned around, he recognized Wyatt's voice, and his stomach lurched with dread. Cody was already furious with him. He didn't want any other member of his team upset with him.

"Should we cancel the party?"

"What party?" Braden asked, flinching as his head

pounded with stress and confusion. The last thing on his mind was celebrating—not until Stanley recovered and they caught the person responsible for hurting him.

Wyatt's face was flushed with embarrassment. "I hate to even bring it up. But Serena and Tammy are throwing me and Fiona an engagement party Saturday night. That's only a couple of days away. And Stanley…"

Might never wake up from his coma. Braden couldn't say it any more than Wyatt could. They all loved the kid too much. Stanley had driven Braden crazy since he'd hired him. He never listened—never did the job exactly as Braden had asked him to do it. But he'd always given his best effort. The kid was all heart.

Someone else had preyed on the kid's sensitivity—had manipulated him into helping hide his identity, into penning those threats so nobody recognized the real perpetrator's handwriting.

Who?

Someone close to all of them. Someone who might show up at that engagement party.

"Don't cancel it yet," Braden advised him.

"But it won't be right if Stanley…" He trailed off. He couldn't say it.

Braden wouldn't even think it. The kid had to recover. Losing acres of trees and a couple of houses was nothing compared to losing him. "He'll be all right, but until he is, well, Stanley wouldn't want you to cancel because of him."

"He's right," another voice chimed in. Cody walked up beside Wyatt and slapped his shoulder. "Don't cancel your engagement party. It's a couple of days away. We'll be celebrating your upcoming nuptials and Stanley's recovery. The kid's tough. He'll be all right."

Wyatt did something the guys rarely did; he grabbed

Cody in a bear hug and embraced him closely. "He'll be all right," he agreed, his voice gruff with emotion. His face reddening with embarrassment, he released Cody and quickly walked away.

That left Braden alone in the hallway with his youngest Hotshot. Like Stanley, Cody hadn't always done what he was told or done it the way he was told to. But he, too, had given Braden his all—his loyalty and his respect.

Braden was worried that he'd lost that now.

"Do it," Cody said.

"What?"

"Do what you said you would—find the son of a bitch who did this to Stanley."

"I will," Braden vowed.

"I know." Cody jerked his head up and down in a quick nod. "I know that's why Stanley had to be questioned. I understand that now. I'm not mad at you."

No. He was mad at Sam. And because Cody was angry with her, everyone else had pretty much ignored her in the waiting room. Was that why she'd left as abruptly as she had? Because she'd known she wasn't welcome?

"I'm mad at myself," Cody said, and his voice cracked with emotion. "How the hell didn't I know what was going on with Stanley? How did I miss it?"

Braden shook his head. "You're asking the wrong man about that..." He hadn't just missed what was going on with Stanley. He'd missed what was going on with Ami and Gingrich and possibly one of his own team. It was good that Sam didn't want a relationship. Braden couldn't trust his judgment.

"I should have noticed something was bothering him—I should have made him talk to me," Cody said.

Braden had thought the same thing about his ex-wife— that he should have noticed she wasn't happy, that he should have known she was going to cheat before she had. But Ami had always seemed happy to him. She had never complained, and neither had Stanley.

"I didn't notice, either," Braden reminded him. "That's why we need to be careful. Whoever hurt Stanley is still out there." He had to be someone they knew—someone else they'd misjudged.

"When we find that son of a bitch, I'm going to kill him!" Cody growled.

Braden caught him now, by the shoulders, and gently shook him. "You're not going to throw your life away— your future with that beautiful woman and that boy who worships you. You're not going to do anything stupid."

Cody sucked in a deep, calming breath. "I know. I know. Serena needs me."

Braden suspected Cody needed her more. He'd once thought he was in love like that—that he'd had a good relationship. But Braden had never had what Cody and Serena had. Until he met Sam…

Now he had that attraction, that overwhelming desire, but he wasn't sure what else they had. He was only sure of what they didn't have—a future. No matter how he felt about her, Sam was focused on her career and her life in DC. She had told him over and over she wasn't staying in Northern Lakes.

"When we catch the arsonist," Braden said, "we're going to make sure he doesn't hurt anyone else."

But Braden was beginning to worry the arsonist already had hurt someone else. Sam hadn't come back inside the hospital, and she'd ridden with him.

Where could she have gone?

17

DAMN MACK. HE WAS always right. About the investigation and about her falling for Braden Zimmer. She'd made two mistakes. One might cost her her heart—the other her life.

She needed to be careful. Whoever the arsonist was, he was obviously willing to kill to protect his identity. Stanley wasn't dead yet, though. At least she hoped he wasn't.

She glanced at the cell phone sitting on her motel bed next to her open laptop. She should call the hospital and check on Stanley's condition. But she wasn't family, so she was unlikely to get any information from the staff. She wasn't likely to get any information out of the Hotshots, either. They all seemed to blame her for Stanley getting hurt. Except for Braden. He blamed himself.

She shouldn't have left him there alone. But he was with all the other Hotshots, so he was safe. She was the one off alone—with a killer arsonist on the loose. She tilted her head and listened. She'd thought she'd heard an engine a little while ago. Now she heard nothing but an eerie silence.

She released the breath she'd been holding and turned

her attention back to her computer screen. Then from the corner of her eye, she caught a shadow pass behind the blinds of her hotel room window. Someone was out there.

She grabbed her gun from her open purse and headed quietly toward the door. She waited for the knob to turn, waited for someone to try to force his way inside. But maybe he had no intention of coming in; maybe he was placing hay bales outside her door instead.

Tightening her grasp on her gun, she pulled open the door. There were no bales on her doorstep—just a hulky shadow looming a door down from Sam.

"There you are," a deep voice murmured as that shadow turned toward her. The light from her open door washed over Braden's handsome face. "They wouldn't tell me which room you were in, but that's a good thing, with the arsonist on the loose."

"You could have called me," she said. She would have preferred a call; she wasn't sure how she could resist him in person.

He looked so exhausted with dark circles beneath his eyes and scratches on his face and arms from the branches. Her heart expanded, filling with concern for him. She wanted to wrap her arms around him and hold him close.

"I could have," he admitted, "but I wanted to see you, to make sure you got back here safely."

He'd been worried about her, too. She hadn't wanted to add to the too many burdens he already carried.

"Yes," she said, "I'm fine."

"How'd you get back here?" he asked. "We rode to-gether to the hospital."

"One of the troopers who came to the hospital for Stanley's statement drove me home." After he'd given up on Stanley regaining consciousness. Another trooper had stayed behind, though. There would be one near Stanley's room at all times, to make sure whoever had hurt him didn't try to finish the job.

"How is he?" she asked anxiously.

Braden shook his head. "No change."

"That's good," she said. "He's not getting any worse."

"True." But his jaw was rigid with tension.

Unable to resist, she reached out and trailed her fingers along his cheek; his dark stubble was rough against her skin. She shivered in reaction, but pushed her own feelings aside and focused on making Braden feel better. "Stanley is young and strong. He will get better."

"I hope so," he said, and how fervently he hoped was obvious in his gruff voice. "But even if he does, he might never be the same. He might never be able to tell us who did this to him."

"I'm working on finding out," she said, gesturing at the laptop on her bed.

He must have taken the gesture as an invitation, because he walked over to it.

Sam shut and locked the door behind him. The room was small, smaller now that he was here. It also seemed to have color where the beige walls, carpeting and furnishings had lacked it before his arrival.

"Is that why you're here?" she asked. "To find out if I've learned anything new?"

He shook his head. "I wasn't sure you were still thinking Stanley acted alone, and maybe just got hurt falling into that ravine."

"He didn't beat himself with that limb," she said.

He sighed. "No, he didn't." As if he were too exhausted to stand, he dropped onto the bed next to her laptop.

"Why are you really here?" she asked him.

He glanced up at her and blinked. For a man, he had incredibly lush lashes, thick and long. "To invite you to an engagement party."

She stepped closer to him and sniffed the air around him. "Have you been drinking?"

He chuckled. "No."

"Then why would you invite me to an engagement party now?" she asked. "Do you think that we're…"

"Dating?" He shook his head. "No. I think the arsonist will be there. It has to be someone Stanley knows, and everyone he knows will be at that party. It's Wyatt and Fiona's engagement party."

She should go—just for his protection. But she still wasn't certain why he'd invited her. "You want me to interrogate the guests? That will go over well."

They already hated her. She didn't care, though; she had a job to do. And once that job was over, she would leave Northern Lakes and probably never see any of them again.

Not even Braden.

Especially not Braden.

If he'd stopped by for any reason beyond issuing an invitation, she needed to tell him to leave. She couldn't be with him again—not physically—because now her emotions were involved, too.

But when she glanced to the bed, she found him slumped facedown into a pillow, breathing deeply. From the dark circles beneath his eyes, it looked as if he hadn't had much rest for a while—maybe since the arsonist's first fire. So it was probably good that he was here, where she could protect him while he slept.

But who would protect her?

Because as she watched him, she imagined how it would feel to share his bed every night. That could only happen in her imagination, though. It could never happen in reality. She couldn't stay. And he couldn't leave his team.

"WHY DID YOU bring her here?" Cody asked as Braden stepped through the door of the Filling Station with Sam on his arm. He'd been asking himself that same question since he'd picked her up at her motel.

That was partly because she looked so damn beautiful in a formfitting silk dress that matched her dark blue eyes. He would have rather stayed in the hotel with her and done something besides sleep in her bed.

That was all he'd done the other night when he'd passed out next to her computer. She'd let him sleep, but she hadn't let him touch her the next morning. She'd already been dressed and on her way out the door when he'd awakened.

He should have been happy she was working the case so hard—that she was more determined than ever to catch the arsonist. But that was the other part of why he wondered what the hell he'd been thinking, bringing her here. If the arsonist was here, this was the last place Braden wanted Sam to be—not that Sam cared what he wanted. She only cared about catching the arsonist. She'd stepped up her investigation.

She'd questioned everyone who'd already been questioned. She'd personally reexamined every piece of evidence. The arsonist had to know she was closing in on him.

But who was he? Braden gazed around the crowded bar. It had been closed to the public for this private party. Only friends and family of Wyatt and Fiona had been invited.

And Sam. But he'd invited her.

"She's my date," Braden said.

Sam glanced up at him, and her blue eyes were a little icy with indignation. She'd made it clear to him it wasn't a date when she'd accepted his invitation. But then she'd worn that dress and had put soft curls in her hair and painted her fingernails...

She looked like she'd dressed for a date.

"Would you rather I leave?" Sam asked Cody.

He didn't hesitate before replying, "No, I'm sorry. I didn't mean that like it sounded. As much as I want you to stop the arsonist, I know you deserve a break. I know how hard you've been working to catch the son of a bitch."

Sam's eyes widened in surprise. "I thought you were mad at me."

He shook his head. "No, I was being a jerk about you questioning Stanley." He glanced at Braden, and there was an apology in his green eyes. "Sorry. Sometimes I can't help but be a jerk, huh?"

Braden chuckled. "Seems that way."

"You're just doing your job," Cody told Sam. "You had to question Stanley. We all tried—every time he was around when a fire started—and he claimed he never saw anything. Obviously he was lying."

"How is he?" Sam asked.

She'd already asked Braden when he'd picked her up, but he hadn't heard the latest.

Cody's mouth curved into a grin. "The swelling's going down and his brain activity appears normal, so they're going to bring him out of the coma tomorrow."

Owen, who'd come up behind them, raised a fist. "That's great!" People turned toward them. "You should make an announcement—bring up the mood of this party."

"It's Wyatt and Fiona's night," Cody said.

"They love Stanley, too," Owen reminded him. "Wyatt wanted to cancel the party. Make him feel better about it."

Sam reached out, as if trying to stop Cody. But he was already moving away through the crowd, looking for the groom-to-be. Owen followed him. She shook her head and uttered a soft sigh.

Maybe she was worried that if the arsonist was here, he might try to hurt Stanley. But she'd already made certain the kid would be safe.

And now he would be well again. "This is good news," Braden told her. "He's going to be okay."

She nodded. "Yes," she agreed. "He will." Her beautiful face was lit up with a smile, as if a light radiated from within her. Despite all the people and the noise, he suddenly felt very alone with her. But not alone enough.

"I shouldn't have brought you here," he said.

Her smile left, and that light dimmed. "I'm sorry. I thought that, too, but now Cody's not mad…"

And because Cody had come around, the rest of the team had, too. Instead of giving her the cold shoulder as they had in the waiting room at the hospital, Braden noticed them looking at her and smiling. But then he couldn't blame them—not with the way she looked.

His heart pounded so fast, so hard, as desire rushed through him. "I shouldn't have brought you here," he said. "I should have locked that motel room door and never let you leave."

His heart stopped beating for a second—with panic— as he remembered she truly would be leaving. Probably soon.

When Stanley came out of the coma, he would certainly tell them who'd hurt him. He wouldn't want to protect someone who'd tried to kill him.

She stepped closer to him and trailed a fingertip

down the buttons on his black dress shirt. The smile and the light were back, but now that smile was a little wicked, curling up just the corner of her lips. The light glinted with naughtiness. "Why do you think I'd try to get away?"

He sucked in a breath. "Maybe I'd be the one trying to get away."

She grabbed his hand. "Where's the bathroom in this place?"

He pointed toward the back. "Down the hall behind the pool tables."

She stepped closer, slid her hand around the back of his neck, tugged his head down and whispered in his ear, "You're coming with me."

He couldn't speak at all; he could only follow silently as she guided him through the crowd. Maybe his team would think he was going outside for some air; there was a door at the end of that hall. But Sam stopped at another door, the one marked Ladies.

This wasn't like Braden. He didn't do things like sneak into the women's restroom. Or have sex on his desk. Or the conference room table…

Hell, this *was* like Braden since Sam had come to town. She'd brought out something in him he'd never felt before—a passion that even he, who tried so hard to control everything, could not control.

He glanced around, but only out of habit. Even if someone saw him, he was going into that bathroom with Sam. His body was so tense he felt like it might snap; he needed her so badly.

She pushed open the door. The room was small—just a single stall, a sink with a long countertop and a mirror behind it. And in the corner was an upholstered chair.

He expelled a breath of relief that it was clean. Usu-

ally the men's bathroom was not. Sam tugged him inside
and locked the door behind them.

"Scared?" she asked him.

He nodded. "Terrified." Because now he knew—
beyond a shadow of a doubt—that he'd fallen in love
with her. And he'd never been so scared.

He'd gone through hell when his marriage failed. But
he didn't think he'd ever felt about Ami the way he did
about Sam. He didn't want to think about how he'd feel
when she left.

But she didn't give him the chance to think. She was
even more desperate for him than he was for her. She
jerked his belt loose and lowered his zipper. Then she
lowered herself to her knees and slid her mouth along
his freed cock.

He leaned back against the locked door for support as
his legs threatened to fold beneath him. Her mouth was
so hot—so wet. Her tongue so soft as it caressed the sides
of him. Then she lifted her mouth and flicked her tongue
around the base of his shaft.

A sound came from his throat—one he'd never heard
himself make before, almost a growl. And he lifted her
from the floor.

"Braden!" She clutched at his shoulders.

But he had her clasped tightly in his arms. He carried
her to the sink and set her butt on the edge of the counter. Then he pushed up the skirt of her dress, moved her
panties aside and eased his fingers inside her. She was
already hot and ready for him.

But he made sure she was anyway, with his mouth
and his tongue. He lapped at her until she let out a cry
of pleasure. She leaned back against the mirror, her face
flushed with passion.

It was all too much for Braden. He fumbled a condom

from his pocket and tore open the packet. His hand shook as he rolled it on. But before he entered her, he lowered his head and kissed her passionately, his mouth moving over hers. He nibbled at her lips, pulling the bottom one between his teeth. She slid her tongue into his mouth, teasing his the way she'd teased his cock. When they pulled away, they were panting for breath.

Then they turned their heads and stared into that big mirror as they pleasured each other. She'd unbuttoned his shirt so she could run her hands all over his chest and shoulders. He'd pushed down the bodice of her dress enough to free her breasts. He flicked his tongue over each tightened nipple.

"Braden…" His name was nearly a sob. She wanted him as badly as he wanted her.

But then he turned her around and lifted her, entering her wet heat from behind, feeling her inner muscles pull him deep. And he thrust gently, in and out of her.

She had to be feeling the pressure that had built inside him, demanding release. He moved faster, drove deeper. She arched her back and hips, meeting his every thrust until she stilled—on the outside. On the inside her muscles clutched at him, then shuddered as her hot orgasm flooded him.

Turning her head, she kissed him, biting his lip to hold in a scream that surely would have brought the Hotshots running to her rescue. But she wasn't the one needing rescue.

Braden was. He was in deeper than he'd ever been—more in love than he'd thought possible. Knowing it was impossible to control his feelings, he let the reins slip free, and he came. The orgasm was longer and more powerful than he'd ever felt. His legs shook a little. Hell, his whole body shook—right down to his soul.

She'd taken that as well as his heart.

He stepped back and stared at her, awed as well as terrified. Her face had been flushed, but now it grew pale. She was shaky, too, as she slid off the counter and righted her clothes.

"We need to get back out there," she said, and her voice shook as well. "Before anyone realizes..."

He nodded, even though he figured it was too late. If anyone had seen them slip off together, they would realize what they'd been doing—especially with how they looked. All her lipstick was gone, but her mouth was still red and slightly swollen from their passionate kisses.

In the mirror he could see his hair standing up in places. And he needed to button his shirt.

"I'll go first," she said, and she was already reaching for the door.

He was getting no kiss goodbye. And he had a sudden realization that that was what this had been: goodbye. He watched in the mirror as she opened the door and slipped out. She was only going back to the party. But Braden had a sick feeling that he might not see her again.

It was similar to his sixth sense for fires. That had ratcheted up, too. Even after that soul-shattering orgasm, his body was tense. He was more edgy now than he'd been before she led him into the ladies' room. And it didn't help that someone knocked on the door.

"Hey, what's going on in there?" a female voice called out. From the innuendo in her tone, he suspected she knew.

But as embarrassed as he was going to be, he had to leave the ladies' room. He had to warn the rest of the Hotshots.

That fire he'd felt coming—the big one—was going to happen soon.

18

WHAT THE HELL had she done? Sam was not the kind of woman who pulled a man—especially a colleague—into a restroom for sex. But she'd been doing a lot of things with Braden Zimmer she'd never done before while working a case. But the worst thing she'd done with Braden was fall in love with him.

Her eyes stung, and she blinked furiously against the tears that threatened. She wasn't a crier. Whenever she'd cried as a kid, her brothers had teased her mercilessly. Crybaby. Sissy girl.

She silently called herself those names now, so she would buck up—so she would remember who she was. She was no-nonsense Sam McRooney. She wasn't a woman in love.

But she had to keep blinking, so much so that she stumbled into someone as she stepped out of the hallway. Small hands caught her shoulders to steady her.

"Are you all right?" a soft voice asked.

Sam blinked away the last trace of tears and focused on the woman before her. The redhead was gorgeous, with porcelain skin and green eyes. But it was her happiness that made her truly beautiful.

"You must be Sam," the woman said as she held out her hand. "I'm Fiona."

"The bride," Sam said as she slid her hand into the woman's surprisingly firm grip. It was good Fiona was tougher than she looked. Sam suspected she'd have to be.

Fiona smiled but corrected her. "Not a bride yet."

"When is the wedding day?"

"We didn't want to set one until the arsonist was caught," Fiona said. "But it sounds like that will happen soon, what with Stanley being brought out of his coma tomorrow."

Sam could surmise what Stanley would tell her. She had a solid suspect now. Did Fiona have any suspicions of her own? The other woman glanced down and smiled again. Then she leaned over and peeled a piece of tissue from Sam's knee.

Her heart stopped for a moment as she remembered how it probably got there, and what she'd been doing to Braden at the time. She loved him so much. Then embarrassment washed over her. Fiona probably knew what they'd been doing. But Sam was more embarrassed she had been so stupid to fall for a man who wasn't yet completely over his cheating ex-wife.

Sam uttered a groan of self-disgust and shook her head.

"Don't worry about it." Fiona smiled. "It's not like Wyatt and I haven't used that bathroom a few times ourselves."

"And everybody calls *me* the slut," another female chimed in as she stepped out from behind Fiona. They were obviously friends because instead of being offended, the redhead laughed. The brunette looked familiar to Sam.

"Tammy!" Fiona exclaimed. "That was rude."

Sam doubted she'd meant the comment for Fiona. She and Wyatt had a future together. Sam was only here to do a job—one for which she had enough trouble getting respect. "It was kind of stupid, though."

"Falling for Braden?" Fiona asked, her brow furrowing.

"How did you—"

"A woman in love recognizes another woman in love," she said.

"You couldn't have fallen for a nicer man," Tammy cheerfully chimed in. "Braden is wonderful."

Sam couldn't argue that. "I'm just here to catch the arsonist," she reminded the other women.

"Is that why you talked to Mandy today?" Tammy asked the question.

Sam remembered running into the other woman outside Fiona's mother's house earlier that day. She'd just been leaving as Tammy headed inside. She'd had her artfully streaked hair in a ponytail, and had been wearing no makeup then. So Sam hadn't immediately recognized her.

Fiona tensed now. "You talked to my mother today?"

Sam hesitated.

"I saw her," Tammy answered for her, "when I stopped to pick up some pictures for the slide show." She gestured to where a slide show of baby photos of the bride and groom played on the wall behind the pool tables.

Sam nodded. "Yes, I was there." Neither had stopped to introduce themselves then.

"Mandy was pretty distracted after you left," Tammy said. "Not that that's anything new for her." She lifted her hand and waved at someone who'd called out her name. "I have to see a man about a shot," she murmured. She kissed Fiona's cheek. "You'll have to piddle without me." Then she moved back through the crowd toward the bar.

Northern Lakes seemed to have a lot of beautiful women. Sam doubted Braden would be alone long after she left. He would find someone in the town where he'd grown up, who would settle down with him and raise the family he wanted. They both had already agreed she was not that woman.

"Mandy's still rattled tonight," Fiona said. Apparently Sam wasn't the only one who addressed her parent by name. "I've asked her what's wrong and tried to talk to her, but she said this isn't the place."

"It's not," Sam agreed.

"I need to know what's going on," Fiona insisted. "Not knowing is going to ruin this night more than knowing."

Sam nodded. "I stopped by to talk to her about your brother. She'd given Matt an alibi for that first fire." But that wasn't all she'd done. When Sam had talked to her, the nervous woman had given her son an alibi for every fire. That bothered her—that the same person claimed to have been with him for every blaze. "Then she added that she was with him for all the other ones." It was too much of a coincidence. But then there was the footage from the surveillance camera—footage that Sam had sent off to a friend at the FBI lab in DC.

"Why would he need…" Fiona trailed off, then nodded in response to her own question. "Because he was furious he didn't get a US Forest Service firefighter position." She blinked now as if she was about to cry. "He wanted to be a Hotshot like Wyatt."

"But he has that felony on his record…"

"Felony?"

"You don't know?"

"My brother and I weren't raised together," Fiona said. "My paternal grandparents sued my mom for custody of me. I've only been back in Northern Lakes a few years. What felony?"

"You need to talk to your mom," Sam said.

Fiona snorted. "I've never been able to talk to my mother. Did you have better luck with her today?"

"No," Sam admitted. Mandy had word for word repeated everything she'd told Braden when he'd interviewed her—as if she'd carefully rehearsed and committed the alibi to memory. For the other fires, though, she'd scrambled.

Fiona shook her head. "Damn her! Damn her!"

"I'm sorry…"

"She's lying," Fiona said. "She wasn't with him when that fire started at the boardinghouse. She was with me. We were shopping for wedding dresses. I'd asked Serena to come along, but she was busy. I was irritated with her until I found out about the fire. Then I felt so bad…"

Fiona shook her head, and her entire body started to tremble. "No, that's not possible. None of it's possible…" All the color drained from her already porcelain skin, leaving her deathly pale.

Wyatt scrambled to her side from wherever he'd been. "What's going on?" he asked, and he shot an accusatory glance at Sam. "Are you interrogating my fiancée at our engagement party?"

"She didn't want to talk about it," Fiona said in Sam's defense. "I made her. I knew something was wrong."

"What?"

"Matthew—it's Matt," Fiona said, her voice cracking with a sob. "He's the—he's the…" She couldn't bring herself to say the word.

Sam couldn't blame her. If one of her brothers had done something so horrible…

Wyatt tensed. "But Braden said there was security footage alibiing him."

And that was why Sam hadn't said anything yet. She hadn't heard back from the FBI lab. After how she'd upset Stanley, she hadn't dared interrogate Matt until she had solid evidence instead of just suspicions.

"I wondered why Mandy started dating the security guard from the hotel," Fiona said. "He is so not her type."

"I thought the footage might have been doctored," Sam said, "so I sent it off to the FBI."

Fiona shuddered. "What has my brother done? What the hell has my family done?" She peered around the crowd. "Where is he? Where's Matthew?"

"I haven't seen him since Cody made the announcement about Stanley improving," Wyatt said, and now all the color drained from his face. "You don't think that…"

Fiona gasped. "He's the one who hurt Stanley. You think he went to the hospital to…"

Finish him off? It was something else no one dared to say but they were all thinking.

Sam shook her head. "He can't," she assured them. "I told the trooper protecting Stanley to only let certain people inside his room." Cody. Serena. Braden…

Braden!

She'd been standing just outside the hallway for a while now, and he hadn't passed her. Where was he? She didn't like that both he and Matt were nowhere to be seen. Had Braden figured it out? Or had the arsonist found him first?

Of everyone he'd targeted since starting the fires, Braden had to be the one he wanted to hurt the most. Braden was the one who'd been on the hiring board, who'd turned him down for the job he'd wanted. Braden was the one who'd dashed his dreams.

After Cody's announcement, Matt had to know it would all be over soon. So he'd want to make sure he took care of the person he blamed for his disappointment. He would want to hurt Braden like he believed Braden had hurt him.

Panic and pain pressed on her heart. Even if he'd never really been hers, she couldn't lose Braden.

So no one would see him following Sam out of the bathroom, Braden had turned the other way when he'd stepped out of the ladies' room. He'd walked down the hall and pushed open the door to the alley.

He needed a moment anyway, to catch his breath and his heart. But while his lungs filled with air, his heart was gone. Sam would take it with her when she left. That would be soon.

Even if Stanley wasn't able to tell them who the arsonist was, Braden had no doubt that Sam was close to figuring it out. She was smart and determined.

Unfortunately, so was the arsonist. He'd eluded Braden for months. But he had to know that it was over; he would be caught. Braden doubted he'd go down without a fight, though.

That was probably why Braden's instincts kept warning him about a big fire. That was how the arsonist would go out—in a literal blaze of glory.

He dragged in another deep breath and coughed and sputtered on gasoline fumes. The alley was only used for deliveries, so it wasn't well-traveled enough to naturally smell so strongly.

There was a truck parked in it now, though. Braden hadn't noticed it right away because its lights were off. He stepped off the stoop at the back door, and that was when he saw the hay bales. They were stacked against the wall next to wooden door to the cellar, beneath the bar, where deliveries were made. It was too late for deliveries now, but that door stood open. And as Braden watched, someone stepped out and reached for a bale—and dragged it into the basement.

His heart lurched. This was it—the big fire he'd felt coming for weeks. From the amount of hay bales, he could tell the arsonist intended to obliterate the Filling Station and maybe the entire block.

Braden hadn't seen the man's face before he'd disappeared again. But he knew who it was. Hell, he'd probably always known. But because he'd had no evidence to support his suspicion, he'd had to look elsewhere for suspects.

He hesitated. Should he go inside and warn everyone to get out? That would take too long—that would give Matt Hamilton time to strike a match. Braden had to stop him before the fire started.

When Matt stepped out for another bale, Braden grabbed him. The kid was big, though—all burly muscles and rage. He pulled easily free of Braden's grasp.

"You are not stopping me now!" Matthew said, his voice a roar of anger and frustration. "I've come too far."

Braden shook his head. "No. No, you haven't, Matt. You need to stop this now before anyone else gets hurt. And we can get you a deal. We can get you the help you need!"

Matt swung a meaty fist at him. But Braden dodged the blow. "You wouldn't help me!" he bellowed. "You wouldn't give me the job I worked so hard for."

"I couldn't," Braden said. "It's policy. If you have a felony…"

"That's bullshit," Matt said. "I was just a kid then. You can't hold that against me."

"I know," Braden agreed. "It's not fair. You were just protecting your mom."

Matt laughed. "That's what she told everybody—that old Bob had hit her—and I was just trying to get back at him."

"That isn't what happened?" Braden asked. He wanted to keep the kid talking until he figured out a way to over-power him.

Matt wasn't laughing anymore. The anger was back—fiercer than before. "No, I was the one he hurt..." His voice cracked, and he sounded like the scared kid he must have been back then.

"I'm sorry," Braden said. "I'm sorry nobody was there to help you then."

"Mom tries," Matt said as he slid one hand into his pocket. His shirt sleeves were pushed up, and there was a bloodied bandage on one forearm. Sweet Annie had bit him—to protect Stanley. "That's why she lied to you. Got her new guy to doctor the security footage. She feels bad over what happened—over the choices she made."

Braden moved a little closer and lowered his voice. "I'm sure you feel bad, too," he said. Matt wasn't a bad kid; he'd just had a rough life—rougher apparently than anyone had known. "And now you have a choice..."

Matt pulled out a lighter and flicked it on. Staring at the flame, he murmured, "No. It's not a choice. I can't stop until it's all over—until this whole damn town is gone."

Braden lunged for him, knocking Matt to the pave-ment. He grabbed for the lighter, flinching as the flame burned his skin. Matt bucked him off and rolled over, stretching out his arm.

And Braden could see what he was reaching for—the gasoline that had pooled beside the hay bales. He knew there'd be a trail of it going down the basement steps to wherever Matt had placed the other bales.

He had to stop him before that flame hit the gas and the building went up. He jumped on his back and shoved his head against the asphalt. Matt grunted but he held his arm out of Braden's reach.

Braden slammed his head down again; he had to knock him out. But the kid was strong. He lurched up and tossed Braden off. He flew back, stopping only when his head struck the Dumpster behind him.

Stars danced in front of his eyes as his vision blurred. Then the stars turned to flames as Matt tossed the lighter into the hay.

There was a whoosh of air as the gasoline fumes exploded. Braden felt the flash of heat against his face. Then he felt the blow of Matt's fist. He struggled for consciousness. He needed to get inside—needed to make sure everyone got out.

But Matt struck him again. This time it wasn't with his fist but with something cold and hard. And despite the flames burning all around him, everything went black.

19

SAM PUSHED THROUGH the crowd. Since most of them were Hotshots, they were tall and muscular. She was too short to see over or even around most of them. She should have gone back to the bathroom right away to look for Braden.

But she'd thought he might have slipped past her and gone up to the bar where Owen, Trent, Ethan and Hank had been doing shots with Tammy. But Braden wasn't among his team.

Before she'd been able to get away, Wyatt and Fiona had shared the arsonist news with the others.

"How could he?" Tammy had asked, shocked that Matt—over probably anyone—had been able to hurt Stanley.

More tears had streaked down Fiona's face as Wyatt had held her.

Owen had just nodded. He seemed to understand that people were capable of doing anything—good and bad. All of them were helping to look for Fiona's brother now. They knew they had to find him before Cody, who'd overheard them.

Sam was the only one looking for Braden. Where the hell was he? It wasn't like him to disappear without a word. He was too responsible—not just for himself but for everyone else as well.

Sam's heart raced with fear, and panic settled in her chest, stealing away her breath. It was so hot in the bar, so smoky…

Nobody smoked in public places anymore in Michigan. And that wasn't cigarette smoke, anyway. She coughed and sputtered as it began to fill the room.

Everyone else was noticing it, too. Shouts and cries emanated from the partygoers. She glanced down and noticed the smoke curling up through the floorboards. Crouching down, she brushed aside some peanut shells and felt the hardwood. It was hot. The fire was beneath them.

"Everybody out!" It was the usually quiet Dawson who shouted the order from where he stood on a pool table. "The bar's on fire!"

No alarms rang out. Maybe the tavern had no working smoke detectors. But somehow Sam doubted that. This wasn't a kitchen fire or someone tossing a cigarette into a trash can in the bathroom. This was arson.

Braden had been right. The arsonist was definitely at this party. But then of course he was; the party was for his sister.

Braden…

While everyone else headed toward the front doors, Sam headed toward the back. A few other people headed that way, too, Maybe there was another way out. Maybe Braden was safe.

Sam blinked again as tears streamed from her eyes. She could barely see through the smoke. So she slid her hands along the wall. She felt the trim as she came upon the door to the bathroom. She had to make sure Braden wasn't inside. Maybe the arsonist had seen them go into the restroom earlier. And after she'd left, he'd struck Braden over the head—like he had Stanley.

Afraid that she might find him lying on the floor in a puddle of blood, she pushed open the door. But the room was empty.

A big hand wrapped around her arm and a deep voice murmured, "That's not the way out."

When she stepped back into the hall, the people who'd been headed that way were turning around. "There's a padlock on the door. We can't get out!" someone said.

If the only other way out was blocked and Braden wasn't in the bathroom, where the hell had he gone? While she hadn't known him long, she knew him well. He wouldn't have left the burning building while she or anyone else was still inside. At least he wouldn't have left of his own free will.

Maybe he was in the men's room. She moved toward where she remembered that door being—she couldn't see anything now. The smoke was too thick. Whoever had grabbed her arm held it yet—as if reluctant to get separated.

"Go with the others," she urged him. As she reached up to pat his arm, she felt something beneath her fingers. It wasn't a shirt; it was a bandage with dried blood. "You need to leave," she said.

"I'm not leaving you here," he replied.

"I need to find Braden."

"I know where he is," the deep voice murmured.

She couldn't see his face clearly through the smoke, but she knew who held on to her. His grasp tightened so painfully she wondered if he would snap her arm like he'd snapped Stanley's.

She held in a whimper of pain, unwilling to let him see he'd frightened her.

"Where is he?" she asked. "What have you done with him?"

Something cold pressed against her palm. A key. "Unlock that padlock and let's step outside and see," Matthew Hamilton told her.

She didn't want to leave with him—especially since she was afraid that Braden might still be inside. But her lungs burned from the smoke, and she was already growing light-headed. If she didn't get fresh air soon, she was going to pass out.

Already the building was beginning to creak. Flames licked up through the floorboards. If she didn't get out soon, she would burn up with the bar. Blindly she fumbled with the lock until it opened and slipped from the hasp.

Matt pushed open the door to the alley. With the fresh air fueling the fire, the flames rose inside—and the floor cracked and dropped into the basement.

She slipped, sliding toward the hole that had formed. But Matt held her arm yet and dragged her out. She was under no illusion he was saving her life. He just intended to take it another way.

IT WAS SO damn hot. Sweat trickled down Braden's brow, running into his eyes like tears. He blinked and wiped at them as he regained consciousness. His head throbbed, and he could feel something sticky against the side of his face. He reached up and touched it, and his fingers came away red. "What the hell...?" he murmured at the sight of his blood.

Then he saw the flames, licking the last of the straw off the pavement of the alley just a few feet away. Flames lapped at the wooden door frame around the opening to the basement as well. He heard a hiss and a crackle and saw the fire leap, rising up through the flat roof of the building. The Filling Station was fully engaged.

In the distance he could hear sirens wailing. The trucks were coming. But they would be too late to save the tavern. Maybe they could stop the fire from spreading down the whole block, though.

Had everyone gotten out?

Had Sam?

Braden tried to stand, but his legs refused to lock beneath him. He slumped back against the Dumpster again. He had to get to his feet—had to get inside that building. Had to make sure everyone got out…

His vision went black as oblivion beckoned again.

Where was Annie to lick his face when he needed her? Damn dog…

Along with the sirens, he thought he could hear her barking in the distance, too. She probably was. Where Serena and Cody were staying wasn't too far away.

But more than Annie, he needed Sam. He murmured her name. And as if that had conjured her, she suddenly appeared—stumbling down the concrete steps at the back door of the bar. She coughed and sputtered and dropped to her knees on the pavement.

Then she saw him, and her eyes widened with shock and fear. "What did you do to him?" she shrieked.

And Braden realized she wasn't alone. A big hand reached down, clutching her tousled curls, to jerk her to her feet.

Rage coursed through Braden, pushing oblivion away. How dare Matt hurt her! He tried to move, but then noticed Sam's finger, pointing at him like he did Annie—wanting him to stay down.

She wanted him to play dead. She wanted to protect him even though she was in danger. She stepped between him and Matt, probably so the kid wouldn't see that he'd moved. "What did you do to him?" she asked again.

Something metal skidded across the asphalt. And Braden saw what Matt had used to hit him: a crowbar. He must have used it to force open the locked basement door.

Matt chuckled. "I always thought Superintendent Zimmer was so tough—that he was tougher than that whole Hotshot team of his—but he went down faster than Stanley did."

"Braden caught you starting the fire?" she asked. She was probably stalling for time.

He could hear the trucks rolling up on the other side of the building. It was only a matter of time before someone circled around to the alley. But he wasn't certain that would be a good thing.

Matt was already behaving like he had nothing left to lose.

The kid snorted. "Must've been that sixth sense of his everybody brags about."

"How he knows a fire is coming?"

"Yeah, he knew—every damn time," Matt said. "He knew sometimes before I knew."

Nausea roiled Braden's stomach. It wasn't because of the concussion he surely had—it was because his premonitions might have caused Matt to set fires.

"I wonder if he knew this was how he would die?" Matt mused, and he pushed Sam aside.

Braden closed his eyes and forced his body to go limp. He would play dead. But he had a bad feeling he might not be playing for long. The building groaned, and smoke filled the alley. The structure was going to collapse soon, and when it did, it would fall on them.

Matt must have realized that, too, because he grabbed

Sam's arm. "We've got to get out of here." He started pulling her toward his truck.

"You can't leave him here," she protested.

"I think it's how he'd want to go," Matt said.

"What about me?" she asked. "What do you intend to do with me?"

Braden wondered the same thing. He doubted the arsonist intended to let her live.

Matt confirmed his fears when he replied, "I have something special planned for you, Hotshot lady arson investigator."

"I'm just doing my job," she said. "It's nothing personal, you know."

"I know," Matt agreed—his voice almost eerily calm. Before he'd set the fire, he'd been full of rage. But now that he basked in the glow of the fire he'd set, he was relaxed—almost at peace. "You should have listened to my warning and just left town. I told you bad things would happen if you stayed."

"Stanley wrote that note," she said.

Matt laughed and shook his head. "No. I just made it look that way. Stanley's handwriting is easy to copy."

The kid was far smarter than any of them had known. He'd set up alibis to protect himself and he'd set up another suspect to take the rap for his crimes. Braden had to make certain Matt didn't leave the alley with Sam because he had no doubt he would never see her again.

20

MATT'S HAND SQUEEZED her arm, pinching the skin and bruising the flesh. As he dragged her toward his truck, she fumbled inside her bag. But she felt only the leather of her wallet, the plastic of a makeup container, the rustle of a crumpled receipt...

She struggled against his hold, finally managing to pull free. Or maybe he got sick of holding her. He slammed her back against the side of his pickup box. She glanced up at him and stared down the barrel of her own gun.

"Looking for this?" he asked her.

He must have grabbed it out of her purse when he'd come up behind her in the bathroom. She'd been so focused on finding Braden she hadn't realized he'd reached inside her bag and stolen her weapon.

Braden...

Was he just playing dead like she'd wanted him to? Or was it for real now?

Matt had hit him with a crowbar. She was surprised it hadn't killed him instantly. But then he was Braden; he had a hard head.

"You're going to shoot me?" she asked. "Is that how you plan to kill me?"

He sighed—then coughed on the smoke that filled the alley. "No. I didn't plan to kill anyone. I didn't even know anybody would be camping when I set that first fire. What the hell were Boy Scouts doing out in the woods so early in the spring?"

She'd grown up in Washington, where they'd camped year-round. But she knew Michigan winters were frigidly cold and long, and that the winter weather usually infringed on spring.

"I don't know," she said, her voice growing raspy as the smoke billowed around them. The burning building creaked as it threatened to collapse.

Braden was too close to it; it would definitely fall on him.

She tried to step back, but she was trapped between Matt and the truck. "What about Avery Kincaid?" she asked. "You tried to kill her."

He shook his head. "I just wanted to scare her. But then she made me mad..." Because she hadn't given him the attention he'd craved. She'd done her special feature about Dawson instead of the Northern Lakes arsons.

"Did Cody Mallehan make you mad, too?" she asked.

"Stanley told me that Cody took the last spot on the Hotshot team—that spot should have been mine." He sounded like a spoiled kid denied a place on the basketball team.

"Is that why you caused his accidents?" she asked.

His brow furrowed. "What accidents?" he asked. "I'd heard he wasn't going to stick around, anyway. He was going to take a job for your dad—smoke jumping."

"Then why did you burn down the boardinghouse?"

"That was to scare Stanley," Matt said. "He started asking me questions. I think he was figuring it out."

So Stanley hadn't been involved. But he had suspected.

"Hey!" someone shouted. "You need to get the hell out of this alley. The building's about to collapse."

She turned toward the end of the alley where a firefighter stood. Even beneath his mask, she could see the bushy beard. Ethan.

Matt swung the gun toward him, then back at Sam. Then finally he pressed it against his own head. Tears streamed from his eyes as he stared down at her. "It's over, huh?"

She shook her head. "No, Matt, it doesn't have to be over."

"I hurt Stanley and Braden. If you arrest me, I'm going to go to jail for a long time—maybe the rest of my life." He shook his head now. "I can't handle that."

But before he could squeeze the trigger, a big hand locked over his. Braden had his other arm wrapped around Matt's neck. Blood still oozing from the wound on his head, he struggled with the younger man. He had to be weak from his injury.

"Get out of here!" he shouted at her.

She was frozen in place—until someone grabbed her. Ethan threw her over his shoulder and headed for the opening to the alley. For such a big man, he moved quickly.

Through the smoke, she could see Matt and Braden weren't moving. They were locked in battle over her gun—both their arms stretched out and straining. Then the smoke thickened, and she couldn't see anything but the glow of the fire as it grew.

The building creaked and moaned, and the flames

roared. But still she heard the gunshot. Ethan lowered her to the sidewalk and someone pressed an oxygen mask over her face. Over the mask she stared into Owen's face. He looked as scared and sick as she felt.

She struggled and dragged the mask down. "Get in there!" she shouted. "Please, save him!"

But she wasn't certain it would be possible to save him. There was more danger in that alley than bullets. With a whoosh of air, the building collapsed—dissolving into a pile of flames and smoke that filled the alley.

There was no escape.

THE FIRE WAS bigger than Braden had predicted. It was hotter. All-consuming. He could smell flesh burning. It was probably his. Or Matt's...

The kid lay somewhere in the alley, burning debris covering him. Like it covered Braden.

He couldn't breathe through the thick smoke. There was no air. Only the heat and the pain.

He wasn't going out like this—wasn't dying in some damn alley. Wasn't dying without telling Sam that he'd fallen for her...

Determination coursed through Braden. With a loud groan, he shrugged off the burning debris and lurched to his feet. He kicked around the rest of the debris, looking for Matt. He found him beneath a pile of bricks and a burning board. The flesh that burned was Braden's as he gripped the hot wood and pulled it from Matt. The kid was unconscious.

Maybe dead...

They would both be dead if Braden didn't get the hell out of the alley. But he couldn't tell which way led to the street. He couldn't see anything but smoke and flames.

Choking, lungs burning, he leaned down and lifted

Matt onto his shoulders. Taking a chance, he headed out—or so he hoped.

Dodging burning debris and pillars of smoke, he wasn't sure if he'd make it, until the smoke finally eased and he stepped in the space between the buildings and stumbled onto the street.

Finally his legs gave way, and he dropped to his knees on the concrete. He couldn't go any farther. The buildings rumbled behind him—like the Filling Station had rumbled before it had collapsed.

Those buildings were about to collapse, too. Braden doubted he could move fast enough to escape them. But then he didn't have to, as his team rushed forward. They helped him to his feet, helped him with Matt.

"Sam…" The smoke had burned his throat so that he could barely speak. "Sam…"

"Sam's okay," Ethan said as he helped Braden toward the EMT van parked at the curb. "She's safe."

Then he saw her, sitting in the back of the vehicle. As Ethan brought him closer, she jumped up and rushed forward. Her beautiful face was smeared with soot, making her blue eyes glisten even more brightly.

She stopped before she reached him and drew back her hands, as if afraid to touch him. "Are—are you okay?" she asked.

He nodded. But he wasn't—because he saw something on her face he'd never seen before. He saw fear.

"I'm fine," he said.

"What about Matt?" Wyatt asked the question as he joined them by the EMT van.

Braden gestured behind him, and noticed the blood oozing from his own charred-looking hands. He'd been burned, hurt badly, but it wasn't the fire that had done it to him. Or even Matthew Hamilton…

Wyatt crouched next to his almost brother-in-law who lay on the sidewalk, Owen leaning over him. Treating him. Hopefully he would be all right.

No, Matt hadn't hurt Braden. Matt had tried to hurt himself. He'd wanted to shoot himself in the head but Braden had wrested the gun from him.

It had gone off. But neither Matt nor Braden had been shot. The building had collapsed on top of them instead. Despite all that flaming debris, it was Sam who'd burned him.

And now she stepped back again, as if she were about to turn and run away from him. She hadn't been scared of what might've happened to him. She was scared of him. Maybe she'd begun to fall for him, too.

But it didn't even matter to her. All that mattered was her career. She moved toward the sidewalk—toward Matt as he began to cough and sputter. He didn't doubt she would get her confession and close her case.

And leave…

Braden should have known better than to fall for her. She'd warned him over and over that she was only in Northern Lakes to do her job. And now her job was done.

21

BRADEN STARED DOWN at the surface of his desk, and as always, images flitted through his mind—images of Sam. A couple of weeks had passed since she'd left, but he couldn't sit in his office without thinking of her—without his body aching for hers.

He'd thought he'd been hurt before, when he'd found out about Ami's cheating. But now he realized that had been nothing compared to what he was feeling now.

He glanced down at the bandages wrapped around his forearms. The burns itched, which meant they were healing. Like his crowbar concussion, those wounds could heal. He wasn't so sure about the other ones—about the hole Sam had left in his heart.

Knuckles rapped against his door. He jumped up and quickly moved around his desk, putting it and all the memories it evoked behind him when he opened the door to Sam's father.

"Hey, Mack," he greeted his old friend. "Thanks for coming so quickly."

Mack ignored Braden's outstretched hand and pulled him into a bear hug. With his barrel chest, the man looked like a bear—albeit one with a bald head. "You should have called me weeks ago."

Sam had still been here weeks ago.

"Your daughter caught the arsonist," Braden said. "That's all over now."

"Sammi?" Mack asked. "Is that what you're talking about?"

"Yeah, you know she's gone." She'd gotten a full confession from Matt—not that she'd needed it after what had happened at the bar—and put him under arrest.

"Is that why you wanted to talk to me?" Mack asked, almost hopefully.

Of course he wanted to talk about Sam. But then that might hurt too much, if all he could do was talk and not see her. Touch her...

"You want me to put in a good word for you?" Mack continued. Then he shook his head regretfully. "Sammi is stubborn. You can't tell her what to do. She's more likely to do the opposite of what I tell her to do."

"She said you asked her to check out the fires," Braden said. "Was that the opposite of what you wanted?"

"That's work," Mack said. "She'll listen to me about work—although I wish she wouldn't have in this case. She could have been killed."

"Matt didn't hurt her," Braden assured him.

"He nearly killed his friend." Sam must have filled him in on the details; she'd talked to her dad.

Why hadn't she called Braden or texted? Just to check on him? Hadn't she cared about him at all? She'd looked so scared...for him or of him?

"Stanley is nearly fully recovered," Braden said. The kid was young and resilient and strong and forgiving. He'd forgiven them for doubting him. He'd even apologized for not sharing his suspicions about Matt sooner.

Shortly after Stanley had woken up, Braden had asked him why he'd suspected Matt.

Stanley had reached down to pet the dog they'd sneaked into the hospital with Owen's help. "'Cause after the fire at the boardinghouse, Annie didn't like him anymore."

Braden had snorted. The dog could flush out arsonists but couldn't learn not to piss in his office. But after she'd saved Stanley's life, he didn't care what she did anymore. "The kid's going to be okay," he told Mack.

Mack nodded. "I know. I've been talking to Cody."

"You're not trying to steal him again, are you?" Braden asked.

"You're the one who stole him," Mack said. "You were only supposed to get him ready for me—give him the experience he would need to be a smoke jumper. You weren't supposed to keep him."

"I couldn't help that he wanted to stay." He wished that Sam had, too. But she hadn't even stuck around to see if he was okay after the fire.

"So what did you want to talk about?" Mack asked.

Braden closed his office door. "Sam uncovered another issue when she was here. Some accidents that might not have been accidents." He'd read through those incident files again, and he had seen what she had. Too many coincidences. And Matt was adamant he hadn't been responsible for Cody's accidents. Just the fires. "I need someone with your instincts to check out my team. Tell me who isn't who they seem to be."

Mack shook his head. "I'm not the man you need for this job."

"Do you have someone in mind?" Braden asked.

Mack's thin lips curved into a smile. "You're the one who has someone in mind. My daughter."

Braden released his breath in a shuddery sigh. Then he admitted, "I can't get her out of my head."

"Do you want her out of your head?"

"No..."

"Then you know what you have to do."

Braden gestured around his small office. "I can't leave here. My team needs me more now than ever." They'd been through hell with the arsons. And if Sam was right, it wasn't over yet. They were still in danger that had nothing to do with the fires they fought. That danger they expected. These accidents were totally unexpected.

And unexplained.

"And I can't ask Sam to give up her career," Braden said. "She's worked too hard to get the position she has. She loves her job." And because he loved her, he could never ask her to give it up.

Mack shook his head, his face twisted into a grimace of disgust. "What the hell's wrong with people?" he asked. "Why does it have to be all or nothing?"

Braden suspected now that Mack was talking about himself—about how his wife had left him. Had there been ultimatums involved? Some of his former team members had gone through that—had been forced to give up their jobs so they wouldn't lose their wives.

"Why can't you find a compromise?" Mack asked.

"How do you compromise kids?" Braden asked. "I want them and she doesn't."

"Did she tell you that?" Mack asked.

Braden nodded. "She's not going to be the settle-in-one-place, stay-at-home mom."

"Then don't ask her to be," Mack said as if it were all so simple. "Find that compromise."

For the first time since she'd left, Braden felt hopeful. He was willing to compromise. But it wouldn't work if

Sam wasn't—if she had no interest in finding common ground on which they could build a life together.

He sucked in a breath, bracing himself. "I'm not sure this is what she wants," he said. "I'm not sure I'm what she wants."

"You won't know if you don't ask her," Mack said. "Don't make the mistakes I made with her mother. I never asked Evelyn to come back. And now I'll never know if she would've…"

"I have nothing to lose," Braden said. Because Sam had already taken his heart with her when she left. He had nothing to lose and everything to gain.

SAM WALKED ACROSS the scorched earth, the ground dissolving into dust and ash beneath her boots. Smoke wafting from the ground burned her eyes, but she blinked quickly, unwilling to close them.

Every time she had for the past two weeks, Sam saw him. Walking out of the smoke like a hero from the pages of some comic book, his arms straining as he carried the man who'd nearly killed him. He'd not only survived the arsonist's fire, he'd saved the arsonist.

She'd been so certain he wasn't coming out of that fire. That he was dead. She'd never felt like that before—had never felt so much fear. Instead of easing when she'd seen he was all right, it had gotten worse; it had nearly paralyzed her.

She didn't want to feel like that—didn't want to love anyone so much that losing him could destroy her. No. She had to focus on her work. On her career.

She wanted nothing to do with love. She'd seen what that had done to her dad. He'd put on a brave face for her and her brothers, but he'd never really gotten over their mother.

Love was scary. Far scarier than any fire or arsonist she'd ever faced. That was why she'd run away the next day. She wasn't proud of herself.

She hadn't even talked to Mack because she knew he wouldn't be proud of her, either. He hadn't raised any of his kids to be cowards. He wouldn't be happy that she'd run away—just like her mother had.

She tried to focus on the scorched ground she walked across, but she couldn't see it. She blinked furiously at the tears burning her eyes. Then she cursed furiously.

"Mack teach you that?" a deep voice asked.

She tensed. "He'd deny it, but it's where I heard it first."

"Case giving you trouble?" he asked.

She blinked again and looked up. The sun was behind him, so he was in silhouette, all hard muscle and dark hair. Maybe she was imagining him standing there. He couldn't be real; he couldn't be here.

"The case?" She shook her head. "No, the case isn't giving me trouble."

He was. She hadn't slept the past two weeks because she'd ached with missing him—with wanting him.

"You've already solved it?" he asked.

She sighed. "Yeah, I think I have." Although the local fire chief was probably not going to be happy to learn his teenage son had been setting the fires. But then Sam was used to not necessarily making friends everywhere she went.

She felt like she'd made friends in Northern Lakes, though. And then there was Braden...

She wasn't sure what she'd made with Braden.

"Good," he said. "I have another case for you."

Fear coursed through her. "Have there been more fires? Is that why you're here?" The town—and the Hotshots—had already been through too much. They didn't deserve any more danger, not now. Not ever.

"No fires," he said. "But a certain investigator found out about some questionable accidents that have been happening to my guys."

"That's why you're here?" She ignored the flash of disappointment. She didn't care why he was here. She was just glad he was.

"Matt denied targeting Cody," she remembered. She'd nearly forgotten that conversation; she'd been too worried about Braden. Too worried about the extent of his head wound and if he'd make it out of the alley...

She shivered.

"You're cold," Braden said. "Is there someplace we can go to get out of the cold?"

It was still just autumn, but the evening air was already quite chilly this far north. That wasn't why she'd shivered, though. Sam knew to dress for the elements—all the elements. But she wished she wasn't wearing a heavy coat and pants right now. She wished she was wearing nothing at all, Braden's naked body pressed to hers.

And a short while later—when she opened the hotel room door she'd led him to—she was. He pushed her inside the room and kicked the door closed. Then he tugged at her clothes, pulling off her sweater and pushing down her pants.

Her hands shook but quickly undid his buttons, snap and zipper, until he stood as naked as she was. It wasn't until all their clothes were gone that they stopped and really looked at each other.

Sam worried he would see more than her nakedness, that he would see her soul. Her love.

She knew she'd given herself away when he'd walked

out of that alley with Matt. There was no way he couldn't know she'd fallen for him.

Was that why he was here? Or was it for this? For sex?

"Sam…" He murmured her name as he reached for her. Then he lowered his head and gently pressed his lips to hers. He glided them across hers in a whisper-soft, tender kiss.

Her breath escaped in a gasp as her heart shifted in her chest, love for him filling it. She stared up at him, awed that he was here. But just to make certain, she lifted her hand to his handsome face and ran her fingers along the edge of his strong jaw. His dark stubble scraped across her fingertips, making her skin tingle. He was real. She hadn't just conjured him in her dreams.

He deepened the kiss. Then he lifted her and carried her to the bed. As he laid her down on the mattress, he asked, "Is this going to be too soft for you?"

"There's a desk by the window," she said. "And a counter in the bathroom."

He lifted her from the bed. And she squealed in protest. "No, no, let's try the bed!"

He sighed. "Seems kind of boring, but whatever you want."

She tensed, thinking of how his ex had preferred car hoods. "What do you want?" she asked him.

"You, Sam. I want you wherever you'll have me."

He couldn't be saying…

No. He just meant sex. That was all he could be talking about. Nothing else was possible for them.

But if this was all she could have…

She was going to enjoy it. She tugged his head down and pressed her lips to his. As she kissed him, she touched him, trailing her fingers over his every rippling muscle.

He was in incredible shape but he was also incredibly made, like a sculpture from granite. All sleek and hard.

The words burned in her throat, but she held them back. Instead of telling him she loved him, she showed him, with kisses and caresses. She pushed him onto his back and closed her lips around his cock.

He growled and lifted her. Then raised her higher, until her legs hooked over his shoulders. And he made love to her with his mouth, flicking his tongue over her clit before moving it inside her.

His hands moved up her body, from her hips to her breasts. He caressed them before rubbing his thumbs over her nipples. Her body shuddered as she came.

Foil crinkled as he ripped open a condom and sheathed himself. Then he lifted her again, moving her lower until his cock nudged her core. He eased inside her, filling her as he thrust his hips up. She clutched at his shoulders and rode him as he bucked beneath her.

Instinctively, they found a rhythm, moving together, and the pressure built within Sam again. She arched her back and touched her own breasts now, rolling the nipples between her fingertips.

Braden groaned. "You are so damn hot. So sexy…"

He lifted his upper torso and took a nipple between his lips, then lightly nipped it with his teeth.

Sam reached behind herself and stroked her fingers between his legs, teasing the base of his cock.

Sweat beaded on his brow. "Sam!" he murmured against her breast.

Then he reached between them and rubbed her clit. And the pressure broke. She rode him fast as the orgasm claimed her. She kept rising up and down as her muscles convulsed and pleasure overwhelmed her.

Braden thrust up again and again before he tensed and

his cock pulsed inside her as he came. He cried out her name and then held her tightly in his arms for a while before finally releasing her so he could slip into the bathroom to clean up.

Sam was overwhelmed by more than pleasure then— she was overwhelmed by love. And she was every bit as scared as she'd been the day Braden stepped out of that alley.

BRADEN HAD ONLY been gone a few minutes. But when he returned to the bedroom, he found Sam scrambling to get dressed. "You're not kidding when you say you don't stay," he said gruffly as fear choked him.

She tensed with her back to him.

"You said you solved this case," he continued. "So you're taking off again?" Was she leaving this town or Braden? He needed to know.

Her bare shoulders lifted in a slight shrug. "I have another case."

"Of course." She was busy; he knew that. "Where's this one?"

"Cute little town in northern Michigan—has a bunch of lakes," she said. "I imagine it's nice in the summer."

Hope warmed Braden's heart. "You'll have to visit and find out."

She nodded. "Yeah…"

"Or you could just move there," he said.

She stiffened.

"I'm not asking you to give up anything," Braden said. "But can't you be an arson investigator out of Northern Lakes? Instead of going back to DC between assignments, couldn't you come back to me?"

"Why?" she asked.

"Because I love you."

Finally, she turned toward him. Tears trailed down her face, which was damp and red. She'd already been crying.

Concern wrenched his heart. "It's okay, baby," he murmured as he pulled her into his arms. "What's wrong?"

"You," she said. "You made me fall for you!" She struck his back lightly with her fist. "You made me fall so hard that I can't imagine my life without you."

"So imagine your life with me," he said.

She shook her head, and her tears dampened his chest. "I don't know how."

"We can figure it out together," he said as he pulled back. Then he tipped her chin up so she would meet his eyes. "Trust me, Sam."

Her lips curved into a smile. "You're the one who was cheated on—you're the one who should have trust issues. Not me."

"Your mom took off when you were a kid," he said. "It makes sense that you'd have trouble believing someone would stay."

"My dad stayed," she said. "He took care of us."

"Good care of you. He raised you to be an amazing person," he said. "That's how I know I can trust you. You have integrity."

"You're a lot like my dad." But she said it like it wasn't a good thing.

He shrugged. "Maybe we have the same sense of responsibility. But we're not much alike beyond that."

"You both try to protect me."

"Because we love you." He brushed away her tears. "I want you to be happy." And if he had to give her up in order to do that, he would force himself to do it. But his arms contracted, and he held her close for another long moment.

She released a shuddery sigh that warmly caressed his chest. "I love you," she said. "So much…"

"Then why did you leave?" he asked.

"I was scared," she admitted. "Scared that I was going to get hurt, and worse, scared that I'd hurt you."

"Sam…"

She pushed her hands between them and eased away from him. "You've already been through too much. You deserve happiness. You deserve that family you want—the kids."

"You really don't want kids?"

She shrugged. "I don't know. I saw how hard it was for my dad."

"Because he was raising you and your brothers alone," Braden said. "You and I would be together—when you aren't working a case. I would never ask you to give up your career."

She drew in a breath and nodded.

"What?" he asked.

"I'll take that case."

"About the accidents?"

She smiled. "I'll take the case to figure out how we'll make this work."

"You will?"

"Yeah, I've solved every case I've worked so far," she told him. "So I'll figure this out, too. I'll figure out how to make you happy."

He kissed her deeply, then assured her, "You don't have to figure that out, Sam. You make me happy just by being you."

The rest didn't matter—if they had kids or not. Hell, even whether or not they got married didn't matter to him now. He knew all that mattered was being together.

Mack was right. It didn't have to be all or nothing. By compromising, it could be *everything*.

She entwined her fingers behind his neck and pulled his head down. Then she deepened the kiss, putting all her passion and love in it. He felt another fire coming, but this time he wouldn't mind the burn at all.

* * * * *

REQUEST YOUR FREE BOOKS!
2 FREE NOVELS PLUS 2 FREE GIFTS!

red-hot reads!

Regan walked out into the chilly night air. A shiver skittered down her spine, but she wasn't sure it was because of the cold or due to being in such close proximity to Jamie. Her footsteps echoed softly on the wood deck, and when she reached the railing, Regan spread her hands out on the rough wood and sighed.

She heard the door open behind her and she held her breath, counting his steps as he approached. She shivered again, but this time her teeth chattered.

A moment later she felt the warmth of his jacket surrounding her. He'd pulled his jacket open and he stood behind her, his arms wrapped around her chest, her back pressed against his warm body.

"Better?"

It was better. But it was also more frightening. And more exhilarating. And more confusing. And yet it seemed perfectly natural. "I should probably get to bed," Regan said. "I can't afford to fall asleep at work tomorrow."

He slowly turned her around in his arms until she faced him. His lips were dangerously close to hers, so close she could feel the warmth of his breath on her cheek.

"I know you still don't trust me, but you're attracted to me. I'm attracted to you, too. I want to kiss you," he whispered. "Why don't we just see where this goes?"

"I think that might be a mistake," she replied.

"Then I guess we'll leave it for another time," he said. "Good night, Regan." With that he turned and walked off the deck.

Her heart slammed in her chest and she realized how close she'd come to surrender. He was right; she was attracted to him. She had wanted to kiss him. She'd been thinking about it all night. But in the end common sense won out.

Regan slowly smiled. She was strong enough. She *could* control her emotions when he touched her. Though he still was dangerous, he was just an ordinary guy. And if she could call the shots, maybe she could let something happen between them.

Maybe he'd ask to kiss her again tomorrow. Maybe then she'd say yes.

Don't miss
THE MIGHTY QUINNS: JAMIE
by Kate Hoffmann, available in February 2017
wherever Harlequin® Blaze® books and ebooks are sold.

www.Harlequin.com

HBEXP0117

Turn your love of reading into rewards you'll love with

Harlequin My Rewards